The Literary Compass: A Guide for English UG Students

EUPHONY – 1

(Prescribed by University of Mysore)

BBA & BCA

I YEAR UG

Author:

Mrs. Krupaliny R C

Assistant Professor of English

Seshadripuram Degree College

Mysore

CLEVER FOX PUBLISHING
Chennai, India

Published by CLEVER FOX PUBLISHING 2024
Copyright © KRUPALINY RC 2024

MANAGEMENT & COMPUTER APPLICATION- SEP-I Semester Syllabus 2024-25

Unit 1 Poems
1. Let Me Not to the Marriage of True Minds- William Shakespeare
2. On his blindness- John Milton
3. A Psalm of Life- Henry Wordsworth Longfellow
4. Digging- Seamus Heaney
5. Self-protection- D H Lawrence
6. Women- Alice Walker

Unit 2 Short-Stories
1. Jimmy Valentine- O Henry
2. The Best Investment I Ever Made- A.J. Cronin
3. The Refugee- K. A. Abbas

Unit 3 Essays
1. On Superstitions- A. G. Gardiner
2. The Light Has Gone Out- J. Nehru
3.Town by the Sea- Amitav Ghosh

Unit 4- Language Component
1. Punctuation
2. Articles
3. Subject-Verb Agreement
4. Prepositions

UNIT 1- POEMS

Sonnet 116: Let me not to the marriage of true minds- WILLIAM SHAKESPEARE

Let me not to the marriage of true minds

Admit impediments; love is not love

Which alters when it alteration finds,

Or bends with the remover to remove.

O no, it is an ever-fixèd mark

That looks on tempests and is never shaken;

It is the star to every wand'ring bark

Whose worth's unknown, although his height be taken.

Love's not time's fool, though rosy lips and cheeks

Within his bending sickle's compass come.

Love alters not with his brief hours and weeks,

But bears it out even to the edge of doom:

If this be error and upon me proved,

I never writ, nor no man ever loved.

About the poet:

William Shakespeare, often referred to as the Bard of Avon, was an English playwright, poet, and actor widely regarded as one of the greatest writers in the English language and the world's pre-eminent dramatist. He was born on April 23, 1564, in Stratford-upon-Avon, England, and died on April 23, 1616.

Shakespeare's body of work includes 39 plays, 154 sonnets, and two long narrative poems. His plays have been translated into every major living language and are performed more often than those of any other playwright. His works span various genres, including tragedies like "Hamlet," "Othello," "King Lear," and "Macbeth"; comedies such as "A Midsummer Night's Dream," "Much Ado About Nothing," and "As You Like It"; and histories like "Henry V" and "Richard III."

Shakespeare's sonnets, including Sonnet 30, are known for their deep exploration of themes such as love, beauty, politics, and mortality. His innovative use of language and mastery of poetic form have had a lasting impact on literature and the arts.

Shakespeare was married to Anne Hathaway, with whom he had three children: Susanna, and twins Hamnet and Judith. Despite the few records about his personal life, Shakespeare's literary legacy continues to influence writers, poets, and playwrights around the world.

Summary of the Poem:

Sonnet 116 by William Shakespeare explores the nature of true love. The speaker argues that genuine love is steadfast and unchanging. It remains constant through difficulties and does not waver with time or external circumstances. True love is likened to a guiding star for lost ships and is unaffected by the ravages of time or physical changes. The sonnet concludes by asserting that if this definition of love is proven wrong, then neither the speaker has written anything meaningful nor has anyone ever truly loved. Essentially, the poem emphasizes that true love is eternal and unshakeable.

In "Sonnet 116," Shakespeare explores the theme of true love, emphasizing its unchanging and unwavering nature. He begins by stating that true love is a union of minds, which is constant and cannot be altered by external circumstances. He declares that if there is any impediment or obstacle that can alter love, then it is not true love. This love is perfect and immutable, unshaken by any challenges or difficulties. Shakespeare makes it clear that genuine love is not dependent on physical appearances or temporary emotions.

Shakespeare continues by comparing true love to a guiding star that remains fixed and reliable, regardless of the storms and changes that life may bring. This star, which he likens to the North Star, is steadfast and provides guidance to lost ships, much like how true love provides stability and direction in life. He also mentions that the value of this love is immeasurable, and it is beyond the comprehension of human beings.

In the final quatrain and concluding couplet, Shakespeare asserts that true love is not subject to the ravages of time. Although physical beauty may fade as time passes, true love endures and remains strong until the end of time, even until the day of judgment. He concludes with a bold statement, saying that if his view of love is proven wrong, then no man has ever loved, and he himself has never written a word. This closing argument underscores the poet's absolute belief in the power and permanence of true love.

This sonnet is one of Shakespeare's most famous and is often quoted for its idealistic portrayal of love as eternal and unbreakable, defying the passage of time and external changes.

Lines 1-2:

"Let me not to the marriage of true minds / Admit impediments."

The speaker begins by declaring that he will not acknowledge any obstacles to the union of two genuinely compatible minds. The "marriage of true minds" refers to a deep and perfect bond between two people.

Lines 3-4:

"Love is not love / Which alters when it alteration finds,"

The speaker asserts that true love does not change when circumstances change or when the beloved changes. True love remains constant.

Lines 5-6:

"Or bends with the remover to remove:"

True love does not shift or bend away when the person loved moves away or leaves. It remains steadfast regardless of physical separation.

Lines 7-8:

"O no! it is an ever-fixed mark / That looks on tempests and is never shaken;"

True love is compared to a fixed beacon or lighthouse that remains steady even during storms and turbulent times. It is not shaken or disturbed by external challenges.

Lines 9-10:

"It is the star to every wandering bark, / Whose worth's unknown, although his height be taken."

Love is like a guiding star for lost ships (barks), helping them navigate. Though the star's position can be measured, its true value or worth is beyond measure.

Lines 11-12:

"Love's not Time's fool, though rosy lips and cheeks / Within his bending sickle's compass come:"

True love is not subject to the whims of Time. Although Time can affect physical beauty (rosy lips and cheeks) with its scythe, love remains unaffected.

Lines 13-14:

"Love alters not with his brief hours and weeks, / But bears it out even to the edge of doom."

True love does not change with the passage of hours or weeks. It endures until the end of time ("the edge of doom").

Final Couplet:

"If this be error and upon me proved, / I never writ, nor no man ever loved."

The speaker concludes by asserting that if the definition of love given in the sonnet is proven wrong, then he has never written anything meaningful, and no one has ever truly loved.

Annotations:
Let me not to the marriage of true minds
Admit impediments; love is not love
Which alters when it alteration finds,
Or bends with the remover to remove.

     Sonnet 116, often titled "Let me not to the marriage of true minds," is one of William Shakespeare's most famous sonnets. In this sonnet, Shakespeare explores the nature of true love, emphasizing its steadfastness and constancy. The opening lines set the tone by declaring that genuine love cannot acknowledge or admit any obstacles ("impediments"). The poet asserts that love, if it is true, does not change when circumstances change ("alters when it alteration finds") or disappear when the beloved changes or departs ("bends with the remover to remove"). Shakespeare uses these lines to argue that true love is unwavering and constant, regardless of external factors. He suggests that love is a fixed point, an unyielding force that remains unaffected by the shifting tides of life. This view of love contrasts with the more cynical or practical views that might see love as mutable and contingent on circumstances. Shakespeare's idealization of love in this sonnet celebrates its purity and permanence, highlighting the belief that true love is an eternal and unchangeable bond between two minds.

O no, it is an ever-fixèd mark
That looks on tempests and is never shaken;
It is the star to every wand'ring bark
Whose worth's unknown, although his height be taken.

In these lines from Sonnet 116, Shakespeare continues his exploration of the nature of true love by comparing it to an "ever-fixèd mark" and a guiding star. The phrase "ever-fixèd mark" suggests that true love is a constant and reliable presence, like a lighthouse that remains steady and unwavering, even in the midst of storms ("tempests"). This imagery conveys the idea that love endures through difficult times and remains unaffected by external challenges.

Furthermore, Shakespeare likens true love to "the star to every wand'ring bark," referring to the North Star, which has historically been used by sailors ("bark") to navigate. The star serves as a dependable guide, even though its full significance ("worth's unknown") cannot be completely measured or understood ("although his height be taken"). This comparison emphasizes that true love, like the North Star, provides direction and guidance, offering a stable point of reference in a world that may be confusing or uncertain. Even though love's full value might not be fully comprehensible, its existence and constancy are undeniable and vital. Shakespeare's portrayal of love as both a steadfast beacon and a mysterious force underscores its timeless and unchangeable nature.

Love's not time's fool, though rosy lips and cheeks
Within his bending sickle's compass come.
Love alters not with his brief hours and weeks,
But bears it out even to the edge of doom:

In these lines, Shakespeare asserts that true love is not subject to the ravages of time. By stating "Love's not time's fool," he argues that love is not at the mercy of time's passing; it does not wither or fade as physical beauty does. The reference to "rosy lips and cheeks" symbolizes youthful beauty, which inevitably succumbs to time's "bending sickle," a metaphor for the scythe of Death that harvests life. This imagery emphasizes the transient nature of physical attributes and the inescapable decay that time brings.

However, true love transcends these temporal changes. Shakespeare declares that love "alters not with his brief hours and weeks," suggesting that genuine love is not fleeting or dependent on the passage of time. Instead, it remains constant and enduring. The phrase "bears it out even to the edge of doom" underscores love's resilience, implying that true love lasts until the end of time, or "doom," possibly referring to Judgment Day or the end of existence. Through these lines, Shakespeare conveys that true love is eternal, unchanging, and unbreakable, unaffected by the ephemeral nature of life and time's inevitable toll on beauty and youth.

If this be error and upon me proved,
I never writ, nor no man ever loved.

In the concluding couplet of Sonnet 116, Shakespeare delivers a bold assertion to solidify his argument about the nature of true love. He states, "If this be error and upon me proved," challenging anyone to disprove his definition of love. By using the hypothetical "If this," he refers to the qualities of love he has described throughout the sonnet—its constancy, unchanging nature, and immunity to the effects of time.

The following line, "I never writ, nor no man ever loved," serves as a powerful statement of conviction. Shakespeare implies that if his portrayal of love is wrong, then it would mean that he has never written anything true, and no one has ever truly experienced love. This assertion emphasizes his confidence in the universality and truth of his depiction. It suggests that the qualities he attributes to love are not merely personal beliefs but are intrinsic characteristics of love itself. The use of hyperbole in this couplet—claiming the non-existence of love if his view is incorrect—reinforces the poet's belief in the enduring and immutable nature of true love. Shakespeare concludes with an unshakeable declaration that true love, as he defines it, is an eternal and unassailable force.

One-word questions and answers:

1. What is the main theme of the poem?
Love
2. What is love described as in the sonnet?
Constant
3. To what celestial object is love compared?
Star
4. What is a metaphor for the passage of time in the poem?
Sickle
5. What does love not do according to the poem?
Change
6. Is true love affected by time?
No
7. What phrase represents the end of time in the poem?
Doom
8. How is love described in terms of its endurance?
Permanent
9. Does true love admit impediments?
No

Long Question and Answers:

1. Discuss the concept of true love as presented in Sonnet 116.

In Sonnet 116, Shakespeare presents a profound and idealistic view of true love. The poem defines true love as unwavering, constant, and impervious to the ravages of time and external circumstances. Shakespeare begins by asserting that love is a "marriage of true minds," suggesting a union that transcends physical attraction or superficiality. True love, according to the poet, "admits no impediments," meaning it remains steadfast and unaltered regardless of obstacles.

The sonnet emphasizes the constancy of love through various metaphors. Love is described as an "ever-fixed mark," akin to a lighthouse that remains unmoved amidst storms. This image conveys the idea that love is a guiding and unshakeable force, offering stability and direction. Shakespeare further compares love to the North Star, a reliable point of navigation for lost sailors ("every wand'ring bark"). The star's value is immeasurable ("worth's unknown"), but its importance as a guide remains undeniable. This metaphor highlights love's role as a dependable and guiding force in life.

Additionally, Shakespeare argues that true love is not subject to time's decay. The poem dismisses the notion that love can diminish as physical beauty fades ("rosy lips and cheeks / Within his bending sickle's compass come"). True love, as depicted in the sonnet, is not "time's fool" and does not alter with the passage of time. Instead, it "bears it out even to the edge of doom," suggesting that love endures until the end of time or existence.

In the final couplet, Shakespeare solidifies his argument by stating that if his depiction of love is incorrect, then he has never written, and no one has ever truly loved. This bold assertion underscores the poet's confidence in his understanding of love's nature. Overall, Sonnet 116 presents true love as eternal, unchanging, and an essential guiding force that transcends the temporal and the physical.

2. How does Sonnet 116 reflect the Renaissance ideals of love and the human condition?

Sonnet 116 reflects the Renaissance ideals of love and the human condition through its exploration of the nature of true love, its constancy, and its transcendence over time and change. During the Renaissance, a period characterized by a renewed interest in classical philosophy, literature, and humanism, there was a deep fascination with the nature of human emotions and relationships, particularly love.

The poem embodies the Renaissance ideal of love as a noble and spiritual connection that surpasses mere physical attraction or fleeting passions. Shakespeare's portrayal of love as a "marriage of true minds" aligns with the humanist belief in the importance of intellectual and spiritual bonds. The notion that love is a union of minds rather than just bodies emphasizes the Renaissance view of love as an elevating and ennobling force. This perspective contrasts with the more cynical or pragmatic views of love that focus solely on physical or material aspects.

Moreover, the sonnet's emphasis on the constancy and permanence of true love reflects the Renaissance ideal of timeless virtues. During this period, there was a strong belief in the existence of eternal truths and ideals. Shakespeare's assertion that true love "alters not with his brief hours and weeks" and "bears it out even to the edge of doom" suggests that love is an unchanging and eternal force, unaffected by the temporal nature of the world. This idea resonates with the Renaissance fascination with the eternal and the immutable, qualities that were often associated with the divine.

The imagery of time and decay in the sonnet also mirrors the Renaissance concern with the human condition, particularly the inevitability of aging and death. By personifying time as a force with a "bending sickle," Shakespeare acknowledges the transient nature of physical beauty and life. However, by declaring that true love is not "time's fool," the poet elevates love above the physical realm, suggesting that it transcends the limitations of the human condition. This elevation of love aligns with the Renaissance ideal of seeking higher truths and values that surpass the mundane aspects of existence.

In conclusion, Sonnet 116 reflects Renaissance ideals through its celebration of love as an eternal, spiritual, and intellectual bond. The poem's exploration of the constancy of love, its transcendence over time, and its resistance to change encapsulates the Renaissance fascination with timeless virtues and the quest for higher truths. Shakespeare's portrayal of love as an enduring and unchangeable force serves as a testament to the period's belief in the nobility of the human spirit and the power of true love.

ON HIS BLINDNESS – JOHN MILTON

When I consider how my light is spent
Ere half my days in this dark world and wide,
And that one talent which is death to hide
Lodg'd with me useless, though my soul more bent
To serve therewith my Maker, and present
My true account, lest he returning chide,
"Doth God exact day-labour, light denied?"
I fondly ask. But Patience, to prevent
That murmur, soon replies: "God doth not need
Either man's work or his own gifts: who best
Bear his mild yoke, they serve him best. His state
Is kingly; thousands at his bidding speed
And post o'er land and ocean without rest:
They also serve who only stand and wait."

About the Poet: John Milton (1608-1674) was an English poet, scholar, and civil servant, best known for his epic poem "Paradise

Lost," which is considered one of the greatest works in English literature. Born in London, Milton was highly educated, attending Christ's College, Cambridge, where he became proficient in multiple languages and classical literature.

Despite becoming completely blind by 1652, Milton continued to write, dictating his later works to assistants. "Paradise Lost," published in 1667, is his magnum opus, exploring the biblical story of the Fall of Man with profound theological, philosophical, and poetic insights. He followed this with "Paradise Regained" and the tragedy "Samson Agonistes."

Summary:

John Milton's poem "On His Blindness" reflects on the poet's struggle with his own blindness and his acceptance of God's will.

The poem begins with the speaker lamenting his blindness, which he describes as a loss of his "light." He feels that his ability to serve God is now severely limited because his talent for writing and creating, which he views as a gift from God, can no longer be fully utilized. This concern leads him to question how he can fulfill his duty to God when his ability to work and contribute seems to be taken away.

The speaker is troubled by the idea that he might be wasting his "talent" (a reference both to his abilities and to the biblical parable of the talents, where servants are entrusted with resources to manage). He fears that God might judge him for not making use of the gift he has been given, even though his blindness prevents him from doing so.

As the speaker wrestles with this anxiety, he realizes that God does not demand work or gifts from those who are unable to provide them. Instead, God values patience and faithfulness. The speaker concludes that those who "best bear his mild yoke" (those who accept their burdens and limitations with grace and patience) serve God just as well, if not better, than those who are actively working.

The final lines of the sonnet express a profound understanding: "They also serve who only stand and wait." This suggests that even in his blindness and apparent inactivity, the speaker is still serving God by being patient and trusting in His will.

"On His Blindness" by John Milton is a sonnet, specifically an Italian or Petrarchan sonnet. The structure of the poem is as follows:

Rhyme Scheme

The sonnet is divided into two parts:

1. Octave (first eight lines): The rhyme scheme is ABBAABBA.

2. Sestet (last six lines): The rhyme scheme can vary, but in "On His Blindness," it is CDECDE.

Meter

The poem is written in iambic pentameter, which means each line has ten syllables with a pattern of an unstressed syllable followed by a stressed syllable, repeated five times.

Structure Breakdown

Octave (Lines 1-8)

The octave presents the problem or situation:

- Lines 1-2: Milton introduces his blindness and expresses his frustration and despair.

- Lines 3-6: He reflects on how his blindness affects his ability to serve God and use his talent.

- Lines 7-8: He questions whether God still expects work from him despite his blindness.

Sestet (Lines 9-14)

The sestet provides the resolution or answer to the problem:

- Lines 9-12: Patience personified replies, explaining that God does not need man's work or gifts; those who best serve God bear his mild yoke and patiently endure.

- Lines 13-14: The final lines conclude that those who patiently wait and bear their burdens serve God just as well as those who are actively doing his work.

Line by line explanation:

Lines 1-2

When I consider how my light is spent, Ere half my days, in this dark world and wide,

- Milton reflects on his blindness ("how my light is spent") which came upon him in the middle of his life ("Ere half my days").

- He describes the world as "dark" because of his blindness and "wide" to emphasize the vastness of the world he can no longer fully perceive.

Lines 3-4

And that one Talent which is death to hide Lodged with me useless, though my Soul more bent

- He laments that his talent for writing, which he considers a divine gift ("one Talent"), is now useless.

- The phrase "which is death to hide" references the Parable of the Talents from the Bible, implying that not using his talent feels like a sin or a waste.

- Despite his blindness, his soul ("my Soul") is even more inclined ("more bent") to serve God.

Lines 5-6

To serve therewith my Maker, and present My true account, lest he returning chide;

- Milton's desire is to serve God ("my Maker") with his talent.

- He wants to "present my true account," meaning he wants to show how he has used his gifts, to avoid God's disapproval ("lest he returning chide").

Lines 7-8

"Doth God exact day-labour, light denied?" I fondly ask. But Patience, to prevent

- Milton questions whether God expects him to work ("exact day-labour") despite his blindness ("light denied").

- He admits this question is asked fondly, or perhaps naively.

- "Patience" is personified and steps in to respond to Milton's question before he can further complain ("to prevent that murmur").

Lines 9-10

That murmur, soon replies, "God doth not need Either man's work or his own gifts; who best

- Patience explains that God does not need human work or gifts.

- God's requirements are not dependent on human abilities or offerings.

Lines 11-12

Bear his mild yoke, they serve him best. His state Is Kingly. Thousands at his bidding speed

- Those who "bear his mild yoke" (accept their burdens patiently) serve God best.

- Patience describes God's authority as "Kingly," indicating His sovereign rule.

- Thousands of angels or followers ("at his bidding speed") serve God actively, doing his will.

Lines 13-14

And post o'er Land and Ocean without rest: They also serve who only stand and wait."

- These followers tirelessly serve God across the world ("post o'er Land and Ocean without rest").

- However, Patience reassures Milton that those who patiently wait and endure their trials ("who only stand and wait") also serve God.

The poem ultimately conveys a message of acceptance and faith, asserting that those who bear their burdens with patience are also fulfilling their divine duty.

Annotations:

1. When I consider how my light is spent
Ere half my days, in this dark world and wide,
And that one talent which is death to hide
Lodged with me useless, though my soul more bent

In the opening lines of John Milton's sonnet "On His Blindness," the poet reflects on his own blindness with a sense of deep concern and resignation. The phrase "how my light is spent" metaphorically represents his eyesight or vision, suggesting that he has lost it. The poet laments that he has become blind before reaching the midpoint of his life, a time he views as a "dark world" because of his impairment. Milton refers to his "one talent," a term that alludes to the biblical parable where talents symbolize valuable gifts or skills entrusted to individuals. Here, however, his talent feels "useless" because he cannot utilize it due to his blindness. Despite his condition, Milton's "soul more bent"—his inner resolve and dedication—remains strong, showing his commitment to serve God. This paradox of having a valuable gift rendered ineffective by his blindness creates a profound sense of personal crisis and frustration.

2.To serve therewith my Maker, and present
My true account, lest he returning chide,
Doth God exact day-labour, light denied?
I fondly ask. But Patience, to prevent

In these lines, Milton expresses his anxiety about his ability to fulfil his divine duties due to his blindness. He desires to use his remaining talents to "serve" God and present a "true account" of his efforts, fearing that he might be criticized ("chide") by God for not being productive. He questions whether God demands labour from him despite his inability to see ("light denied"), reflecting his concern that he cannot meet divine expectations due to his condition. The term "fondly ask" indicates that Milton realizes his question may be misguided or naïve. He turns to "Patience" for reassurance, suggesting that he hopes patience will provide the answer or alleviate his worries about his perceived inadequacy. This transition highlights Milton's internal struggle and his search for solace in accepting his limitations.

3.That murmur, soon replies, "God doth not need
Either man's work or his own gifts. Who best

Bear his mild yoke, they serve him best. His state
Is kingly: thousands at his bidding speed

In these lines, Patience responds to Milton's concerns with a comforting revelation. She explains that God does not require human work or personal talents to achieve His divine purposes. Instead, what matters most is the ability to endure and accept God's "mild yoke" with humility and patience. The "mild yoke" symbolizes the burdens or challenges God sets before individuals, and those who bear these burdens with grace and patience are considered to serve Him best. Patience underscores that God's "state" or realm is majestic and sovereign, described as "kingly." In this divine kingdom, countless beings carry out God's will effortlessly and without rest. This perspective reassures Milton that his value in serving God is not diminished by his blindness, but rather by his attitude and acceptance.

4.And post o'er land and ocean without rest:
They also serve who only stand and wait.

In these concluding lines, Patience extends her reassurance by emphasizing the vast scale of divine service. The phrase "post o'er land and ocean without rest" refers to the countless beings, such as angels or messengers, who tirelessly fulfil God's commands across the world. They serve God by carrying out His will incessantly and without fatigue.

The final line, "They also serve who only stand and wait," delivers a key message of the sonnet. It reassures Milton that even those who cannot actively engage in work or labour, but who instead endure and patiently wait, are still serving God. This sentiment suggests that the value of service is not solely measured by active work, but also by the virtue of patience and steadfastness in the face of hardship. This realization helps Milton accept his blindness and find peace in the notion that his silent patience is a form of service in itself.

One-word question and answers:
1. What is the main theme of the sonnet?
   Patience
2. Who is the speaker of the sonnet?
   Milton
3. What emotion does Milton primarily express in the sonnet?
   Despair
4. How does Milton resolve his struggle in the sonnet?
   Acceptance
5. What does God expect from Milton despite his blindness?
   Patience
6. How does Milton feel about his talent in the context of his blindness?
   Useless
7. How is God's realm described in the sonnet?
   Kingly
8. What is considered a form of service to God in the sonnet?
   Patience

Long Question and Answers:

1. How does Milton use the theme of blindness to explore the concept of personal and spiritual fulfilment?

In "On His Blindness," Milton uses his personal experience of blindness as a metaphor for spiritual struggle and the quest for fulfilment. The sonnet reflects Milton's concern about his inability to use his talents due to his blindness and his fear of not being able to serve God effectively. As he contemplates his condition, he initially feels that his blindness renders his life and work useless. However, through the dialogue with Patience, Milton comes to understand that true service to God is not confined to active work but also includes the acceptance of one's limitations with patience and faith. This realization allows Milton to find spiritual fulfilment despite his physical impairment, suggesting that inner virtue and resilience are more significant in serving a higher purpose than outward accomplishments.

2. What role does Patience play in the resolution of Milton's internal conflict in the sonnet?

Patience plays a crucial role in resolving Milton's internal conflict by providing a perspective that alleviates his fears and frustrations. As Milton struggles with the idea that his blindness might prevent him from fulfilling his divine duties, Patience reassures him that God does not require human work or talents for His purposes. Instead, she emphasizes that enduring God's "mild yoke" with patience is a form of service that is valued by God. This shift in perspective helps Milton understand that his value lies in his attitude towards his suffering rather than in his physical ability to perform tasks. Patience's guidance leads him to accept his condition and find peace, recognizing that even those who cannot actively work but who wait with faith are serving God.

3. Discuss how Milton's sonnet reflects the broader philosophical and theological ideas of his time.

Milton's sonnet reflects the broader philosophical and theological ideas of the 17th century, particularly those concerning the nature of divine providence and human purpose. During Milton's time, there was a strong emphasis on the idea of individual duty and service to God, often framed within the context of productivity and active engagement. Milton's exploration of his own blindness and perceived inability to contribute reflects the tension between personal limitations and spiritual expectations. The sonnet aligns with the Calvinistic notion of predestination and divine will, suggesting that God's purposes are not contingent on human actions but on the acceptance of one's role in the divine plan. Additionally, the idea that patience and endurance are valuable forms of service resonates with the Christian understanding of suffering and redemption, emphasizing that spiritual worth is found in one's inner disposition and faith rather than in outward achievements.

***

A PSLAM OF LIFE – HENRY WORDSWORTH LONGFELLOW

What The Heart Of The Young Man Said To The Psalmist.

Tell me not, in mournful numbers,
   Life is but an empty dream!
For the soul is dead that slumbers,
   And things are not what they seem.

Life is real! Life is earnest!
   And the grave is not its goal;
Dust thou art, to dust returnest,
   Was not spoken of the soul.

Not enjoyment, and not sorrow,
   Is our destined end or way;
But to act, that each to-morrow
   Find us farther than to-day.

Art is long, and Time is fleeting,
   And our hearts, though stout and brave,
Still, like muffled drums, are beating
   Funeral marches to the grave.

In the world's broad field of battle,
   In the bivouac of Life,

Be not like dumb, driven cattle!
Be a hero in the strife!

Trust no Future, howe'er pleasant!
Let the dead Past bury its dead!
Act,— act in the living Present!
Heart within, and God o'erhead!

Lives of great men all remind us
We can make our lives sublime,
And, departing, leave behind us
Footprints on the sands of time;

Footprints, that perhaps another,
Sailing o'er life's solemn main,
A forlorn and shipwrecked brother,
Seeing, shall take heart again.

Let us, then, be up and doing,
With a heart for any fate;
Still achieving, still pursuing,
Learn to labor and to wait.

Summary:

The poem "A Psalm of Life" is an inspirational and motivational piece that encourages readers to live life with purpose and vigor. Longfellow uses the poem to deliver a powerful message about the value of living a meaningful and active life.

The poem begins with a call to action, urging individuals not to be passive or resigned but to actively engage in life and make the most of their time. Longfellow emphasizes that life is brief and should not be wasted in idle reflection or despair. He rejects the idea of life as a mere "dream" and instead advocates for an approach filled with energy and resolve.

The central theme of the poem is the importance of living a life of purpose and action. Longfellow encourages readers to embrace challenges and strive to leave a lasting impact. He uses vivid imagery to illustrate that life is a battlefield where one must fight with determination and courage. The poem stresses that individuals should live authentically, pursue their goals with passion, and not be deterred by difficulties.

Longfellow also contrasts the lives of those who merely exist versus those who live with purpose and conviction. He suggests that while life can be challenging, it is crucial to face these challenges with fortitude and hope. The poem concludes with an uplifting call to live a life that is meaningful and impactful, reflecting the idea that individuals should strive to achieve greatness and make a difference.

Overall, "A Psalm of Life" serves as a rallying cry for readers to take an active role in shaping their destinies and to approach life with a spirit of optimism and determination.

Annotations:

Tell me not, in mournful numbers,
Life is but an empty dream!
For the soul is dead that slumbers,
And things are not what they seem.

In these opening lines of Henry Wadsworth Longfellow's poem "A Psalm of Life," the speaker dismisses a pessimistic view of life as merely an "empty dream." He critiques the idea that life is meaningless or insubstantial, asserting that such a perspective is misguided. The phrase "Tell me not, in mournful numbers" reflects his rejection of sorrowful or defeatist portrayals of existence. He emphasizes that a person who remains passive or inactive—who metaphorically "slumbers"—is spiritually lifeless. According to the speaker, true vitality comes from active engagement in life, not from passivity. Furthermore, he suggests that appearances can be deceptive, and life is not as superficial or meaningless as it might seem at first glance. The lines thus set the stage for the poem's message, which advocates for living with purpose and vigor.

In the world's broad field of battle,
In the bivouac of Life,
Be not like dumb, driven cattle!
Be a hero in the strife!

In these lines from "A Psalm of Life," Longfellow uses vivid military imagery to convey his message about how to approach life. He describes life as a "broad field of battle" and a "bivouac," suggesting that it is a place of ongoing struggle and temporary challenges. Instead of passively following the crowd like "dumb, driven cattle," which symbolizes a lack of direction and purpose, the speaker urges individuals to take an active and courageous role. By advocating for readers to "be a hero in the strife," Longfellow emphasizes the importance of confronting life's difficulties with bravery and initiative. This call to action reinforces the poem's central theme: living with purpose and determination rather than succumbing to passivity or resignation.

Footprints, that perhaps another,
*   Sailing o'er life's solemn main,*
A forlorn and shipwrecked brother,
*   Seeing, shall take heart again.*

In these lines of "A Psalm of Life," Longfellow employs a metaphor of a journey across a "solemn main," or the sea, to illustrate the impact of one's actions on others. The "footprints" left behind symbolize the deeds and example set by individuals as they navigate through life's challenges. The speaker suggests that these actions can inspire and uplift others who are struggling. Specifically, a "forlorn and shipwrecked brother"—someone who is despondent and lost, like a shipwrecked sailor—might find renewed hope and courage by observing the positive example left by those who have faced similar trials. The imagery of the shipwrecked brother highlights the potential for one's efforts to provide solace and encouragement to others who are in need, reinforcing the poem's message that living a life of purpose and resilience can have a profound and uplifting effect on those around us.

One- word question and answers:

1. What is the central theme of the poem?
   Action
2. How is life portrayed in the poem?
   Battle
3. What does the speaker urge readers to be?
   Heroic
4. What metaphor is used to describe life's struggles?
   Battlefield
5. What should individuals avoid being like?
   Cattle
6. What is the effect of positive actions on others?
   Inspiration
7. How is the sea described in the metaphor?
   Solemn
8. What is the result of setting a positive example?
   Encouragement

Long Question and Answers:

1. How does Longfellow use metaphors to convey his message about living a purposeful life in "A Psalm of Life"?

In "A Psalm of Life," Longfellow employs powerful metaphors to emphasize the importance of living with purpose and determination. He describes life as a "broad field of battle" and a "bivouac," portraying it as a realm of continuous struggle and temporary challenges. This imagery suggests that life is not a passive experience but a series of battles that require active engagement and courage. By contrasting this with the image of "dumb, driven cattle," Longfellow highlights the need for individuals to act with agency and resolve rather than merely following the crowd without direction. Additionally, he uses the metaphor of "footprints" left behind in the "solemn main" (the sea) to illustrate how one's actions can provide guidance and inspiration to others who are struggling. These metaphors collectively reinforce the poem's central message: living a purposeful life involves embracing challenges, taking proactive steps, and leaving a positive legacy for others to follow.

2. What is the significance of the call to heroism in Longfellow's "A Psalm of Life," and how does it relate to the poem's overall theme?

The call to heroism in Longfellow's "A Psalm of Life" is central to the poem's overall theme of living with purpose and resilience. The speaker urges readers to "be a hero in the strife," advocating for an active and courageous approach to life's challenges. This call to heroism signifies the importance of not merely existing but actively engaging in life's struggles with determination and valour. The idea of heroism contrasts sharply with the passive existence symbolized by "dumb, driven cattle," emphasizing that true fulfilment comes from facing difficulties head-on and making a meaningful impact. By promoting the idea that individuals should strive to be heroic in their actions, Longfellow underscores the poem's broader message: life should be lived with conviction, purpose, and a willingness to confront and overcome obstacles. The call to heroism serves as both an inspiration and a guide, encouraging readers to approach their lives with courage and intent.

3. How does the poem's message about leaving a positive legacy reflect Longfellow's views on the impact of individual actions?

In "A Psalm of Life," Longfellow's message about leaving a positive legacy reflects his belief in the profound impact that individual actions can have on others. The poem suggests that one's deeds and example can serve as a source of inspiration and encouragement for those who come after. The imagery of "footprints" left in the "solemn main" symbolizes the lasting influence of one's actions. According to the poem, a "forlorn and shipwrecked brother"—someone struggling and feeling lost—may find hope and renewed strength by observing the positive example set by others. This reflects Longfellow's view that personal actions, whether large or small, can significantly affect others and provide guidance through challenging times. By highlighting the potential for one's efforts to uplift and inspire others, Longfellow emphasizes the importance of living a life that is not only purposeful but also considerate of its impact on those around us.

***

DIGGING-SEAMUS HEANEY

Between my finger and my thumb
The squat pen rests; snug as a gun.

Under my window, a clean rasping sound
When the spade sinks into gravelly ground:
My father, digging. I look down

Till his straining rump among the flowerbeds
Bends low, comes up twenty years away
Stooping in rhythm through potato drills
Where he was digging.

The coarse boot nestled on the lug, the shaft
Against the inside knee was levered firmly.
He rooted out tall tops, buried the bright edge deep
To scatter new potatoes that we picked,
Loving their cool hardness in our hands.

By God, the old man could handle a spade.
Just like his old man.

My grandfather cut more turf in a day
Than any other man on Toner's bog.
Once I carried him milk in a bottle
Corked sloppily with paper. He straightened up
To drink it, then fell to right away
Nicking and slicing neatly, heaving sods
Over his shoulder, going down and down
For the good turf. Digging.

The cold smell of potato mould, the squelch and slap
Of soggy peat, the curt cuts of an edge
Through living roots awaken in my head.
But I've no spade to follow men like them.

Between my finger and my thumb
The squat pen rests.
I'll dig with it.

About the Poet: Seamus Heaney (1939-2013) was an Irish poet,
playwright, translator, and lecturer, widely regarded as one of the

greatest poets of the 20th century. He was born in Northern Ireland and grew up on a farm, an experience that deeply influenced his poetry. Heaney's work often explores themes of nature, rural life, Irish identity, and political struggles.

He gained international acclaim for his collections such as "Death of a Naturalist" (1966), "North" (1975), and "Field Work" (1979). Heaney was awarded the Nobel Prize in Literature in 1995 for his lyrical poetry, which "exalts everyday miracles and the living past." His poetry is known for its evocative language, rich imagery, and deep engagement with history and culture.

Apart from poetry, Heaney also translated classic works of literature and was a respected literary critic. His writing style combines the personal with the universal, reflecting on the complexities of human experience while celebrating the beauty of the natural world.

Stanza 1:

**"Between   my   finger   and   my   thumb
The squat pen rests; snug as a gun."**

The poem begins with the speaker holding a pen between his fingers. The pen is described as "snug as a gun," suggesting a sense of power or potential in the act of writing. This comparison also foreshadows the tension between the pen (a symbol of the poet's craft) and the spade (a symbol of manual labor), which will be explored throughout the poem.

Stanza 2:

**"Under   my   window,   a   clean   rasping   sound
When   the   spade   sinks   into   gravelly   ground:
My father, digging. I look down"**

The speaker hears the sound of a spade cutting through the ground, which immediately brings his father to mind. The image of his father digging outside the window creates a connection between the present moment and the past. The word "rasping" conveys the rough, gritty nature of the work, emphasizing the physical labor involved.

Stanza 3:

"Till his straining rump among the flowerbeds
Bends low, comes up twenty years away
Stooping in rhythm through potato drills
Where he was digging."

In this stanza, the speaker's memory shifts from the present to the past. He remembers his father working in the potato fields, bent over with the effort of digging. The "straining rump" and the "rhythm" of his movements highlight the strenuous, repetitive nature of the work. The father's dedication to the task is clear, and it spans across time, connecting the present to the past.

Stanza 4:

"The coarse boot nestled on the lug, the shaft
Against the inside knee was levered firmly.
He rooted out tall tops, buried the bright edge deep
To scatter new potatoes that we picked,
Loving their cool hardness in our hands."

The speaker describes the technique his father used to dig up potatoes. The imagery here is vivid: the "coarse boot" and the "bright edge" of the spade illustrate the precision and skill involved in the labor. The mention of "cool hardness" emphasizes the tangible, physical satisfaction of the work, as the speaker and others pick the newly unearthed potatoes. This stanza conveys a sense of admiration for the father's expertise and the tactile connection to the earth.

Stanza 5:

"By God, the old man could handle a spade.
Just like his old man."

The speaker expresses deep admiration for his father's skill, recognizing that this ability was passed down from his grandfather. The repetition of "old man" underscores the generational connection, highlighting the continuity of this labor across time.

Stanza 6:

"My grandfather cut more turf in a day
Than any other man on Toner's bog.
Once I carried him milk in a bottle
Corked sloppily with paper. He straightened up
To drink it, then fell to right away
Nicking and slicing neatly, heaving sods
Over his shoulder, going down and down
For the good turf. Digging."

The speaker shifts his focus to his grandfather, who was renowned for his ability to cut turf (peat) from the bog. The grandfather's work is described in precise detail, emphasizing his efficiency and expertise. The image of the speaker as a child, bringing his grandfather milk, adds a personal, familial touch. The grandfather's relentless work ethic is evident as he quickly returns to his task after drinking the milk. The repetition of "digging" reinforces the theme of labor passed down through generations.

Stanza 7:

"The cold smell of potato mould, the squelch and slap
Of soggy peat, the curt cuts of an edge
Through living roots awaken in my head.
But I've no spade to follow men like them."

The speaker vividly recalls the sensory experiences associated with digging—the smell of the soil, the sounds of the spade cutting through the earth. These memories are powerful, but the speaker acknowledges that he does not have a spade to follow in the footsteps of his father and grandfather. This line marks a turning point in the poem, as the speaker begins to differentiate himself from the laborers in his family.

Stanza 8:

**"Between   my   finger   and   my   thumb
The   squat   pen   rests.
I'll dig with it."**

The poem ends with the speaker returning to the present moment, holding his pen once again. He resolves to "dig" with his pen, symbolizing his choice to engage in intellectual and creative labor rather than physical labor. The act of writing becomes his way of connecting to his heritage, "digging" into his memories and experiences to create something meaningful.

In summary, "Digging" by Seamus Heaney is a meditation on the poet's relationship with his family's farming tradition and his decision to pursue writing. The poem explores the physicality of manual labor, the admiration for the skill of his forefathers, and the poet's choice to honor that legacy through his own craft.

Summary:

The poem "Digging" by Seamus Heaney is a reflection on the poet's relationship with his family's farming tradition and his decision to pursue writing instead of following in his father's and grandfather's footsteps as a laborer.

The poem begins with Heaney describing his father and grandfather, who were skilled at digging and working the land. Heaney admires their expertise and recalls the sound of their spades "sinking into gravelly ground." He contrasts their physical prowess with his own pen, stating that he will use it to "dig" in a different way—through writing.

Heaney then describes his own memories of childhood, watching his father digging in the flowerbeds. He captures the rhythmic and methodical nature of digging, likening it to the steady beat of the "rasping sound" made by the spade.

As the poem progresses, Heaney reflects on his decision to become a poet rather than a laborer. He acknowledges the skill and hard work required for both pursuits but emphasizes that his "tool" is different—the pen. He sees himself following a different path, one that involves digging into his memories and experiences through writing.

The poem concludes with Heaney affirming his identity as a writer, rooted in his family's farming tradition but choosing to honor it in his own way. He values both his literary heritage and his familial roots, finding a connection between the physical labor of digging and the intellectual labor of writing.

Overall, "Digging" is a poem that explores themes of tradition, family legacy, and the poet's journey to find his own voice amidst the expectations of his heritage.

Annotation:

1. "Between my finger and my thumb
The squat pen rests; snug as a gun."
        The lines "Between my finger and my thumb / The squat pen rests; snug as a gun." from Seamus Heaney's poem "Digging" are rich in imagery and symbolism.

The poet uses the image of a pen held between his finger and thumb to set the stage for the contrast between his own work (writing) and the manual labor of his ancestors. The pen is described as "squat," suggesting it is short and thick, giving it a sense of solidity and substance.

The pen is compared to a gun using the simile "snug as a gun." This comparison introduces a sense of power and precision in the act of writing. Just as a gun can be a powerful tool, the pen, in the poet's hand, is a powerful instrument for expression and creativity.

The pen symbolizes the poet's craft—writing—which contrasts with the spade that his father and grandfather used for digging. While they engaged in physical labour, the poet engages in intellectual labour, "digging" into his thoughts and memories with his pen.

The tone in these lines is reflective and determined. The comparison to a gun suggests that the poet views his work with seriousness and purpose, indicating that writing is his way of contributing to his family's legacy, albeit in a different form.

These lines foreshadow the poem's central theme of digging—both literal and metaphorical. While his ancestors dug into the earth, the poet will dig into the past and into his own experiences through the act of writing.

2. "By God, the old man could handle a spade.
   Just like his old man."
                    The lines "By God, the old man could handle a spade. / Just like his old man." from Seamus Heaney's poem "Digging" are significant for their expression of admiration and acknowledgment of generational continuity.

The speaker expresses deep admiration and respect for his father's skill with the spade. The exclamation "By God" emphasizes the speaker's awe at his father's proficiency, suggesting that the ability to work the land with such expertise is almost revered.

The phrase "Just like his old man" highlights the generational continuity in the family's tradition of manual labour. The speaker acknowledges that his father's skill was passed down from his grandfather, indicating that this knowledge and ability have been inherited and maintained across generations.

These lines underscore the theme of heritage, emphasizing the importance of family traditions and the passing down of skills from one generation to the next. The poem reflects on the pride associated with this legacy, even as the speaker himself chooses a different path.

The use of colloquial language ("the old man") adds a personal and informal tone to the poem, making the relationship between the speaker and his father feel intimate and familiar. This choice of words also reflects the speaker's connection to his rural roots.

While the speaker acknowledges his father's and grandfather's abilities with a spade, he also implicitly reflects on his own choice to "handle" a different tool—the pen. The contrast between the physical labour of his ancestors and his own intellectual labor is central to the poem's exploration of identity.

One-word question and answers:

1. **Question:** What tool does the speaker hold at the beginning of the poem?
   - **Answer:** Pen
2. **Question:** What does the speaker compare the pen to?
   - **Answer:** Gun
3. **Question:** What sound does the speaker hear under the window?
   - **Answer:** Rasping
4. **Question:** What task is the speaker's father performing?
   - **Answer:** Digging
5. **Question:** What crop is mentioned in the poem?
   - **Answer:** Potatoes

6. **Question:** What does the speaker's grandfather cut in the bog?
   - o **Answer:** Turf
7. **Question:** What does the speaker bring to his grandfather?
   - o **Answer:** Milk
8. **Question:** Which sense is evoked by the "cold smell of potato mould"?
   - o **Answer:** Smell
9. **Question:** What does the speaker resolve to use instead of a spade?
   - o **Answer:** Pen
10. **Question:** What does the speaker say he will do with the pen?
    - o **Answer:** Dig

Long question and answers:

1. Discuss how Seamus Heaney explores the theme of heritage and identity in the poem "Digging." How does he use imagery, symbolism, and structure to convey his connection to his family's past and his own path as a writer?

In "Digging," Seamus Heaney explores the theme of heritage and identity through a reflection on his family's history of manual labour and his own choice to pursue a career in writing. The poem delves into the poet's complex relationship with his roots, using rich imagery, symbolism, and a carefully crafted structure to convey the tension between honoring his ancestry and forging his own path.

Heritage and Family Legacy:

Heaney begins the poem by drawing a parallel between his own work as a writer and the physical labor of his father and grandfather. The title "Digging" itself is a powerful metaphor that connects the manual labor of his ancestors with the intellectual labor of writing.

Heaney's father and grandfather were farmers, skilled in the art of digging—whether it be digging up potatoes or cutting turf from a bog. The poet expresses deep admiration for their expertise, as seen in the lines, "By God, the old man could handle a spade. / Just like his old man." This line reflects the generational continuity of hard work and skill, highlighting the pride the speaker feels in his family's legacy.

Imagery and Sensory Details:

Heaney uses vivid imagery to bring the physical labor of his father and grandfather to life. The poem is filled with sensory details that evoke the texture, sound, and smell of the earth. For example, the "clean rasping sound" of the spade sinking into the ground, and the "cold smell of potato mould" create a strong sense of place and connect the reader to the physicality of the work. These images not only paint a picture of the labor itself but also serve to deepen the speaker's connection to his past. The tactile imagery of "cool hardness" of the potatoes and the "squelch and slap" of the soggy peat emphasize the tangible, hands-on nature of his ancestors' work.

Symbolism:

Throughout the poem, Heaney employs symbolism to juxtapose the tools of his ancestors' trade—the spade and the turf cutter—with his own tool, the pen. The spade is a powerful symbol of manual labor, representing the strength, skill, and dedication of the poet's forebears. In contrast, the pen symbolizes Heaney's craft as a writer. The line "The squat pen rests; snug as a gun" suggests that the pen is as powerful a tool in the poet's hands as the spade was in his father's. This comparison underscores the idea that while the poet's work may differ from that of his ancestors, it is no less valuable or impactful.

Structure and Form:

The poem's structure also plays a crucial role in conveying its themes. "Digging" is written in free verse, which gives it a natural, conversational tone. This lack of a strict rhyme scheme or meter reflects the organic nature of the speaker's thoughts as he reflects on his past and present. The poem's enjambment, where lines run on without terminal punctuation, creates a flowing, continuous rhythm that mirrors the ongoing nature of the speaker's connection to his heritage. This structure allows Heaney to move fluidly between memories of his father and grandfather and his current position as a writer, emphasizing the seamless link between past and present.

Conflict and Resolution:

A central tension in the poem is the speaker's internal conflict between following in his family's footsteps and choosing his own path. Heaney acknowledges the value of his family's tradition of digging, but he also recognizes that his own talents lie elsewhere. This is encapsulated in the line, "But I've no spade to follow men like them." Here, Heaney admits that he cannot continue the physical labor of his ancestors, but he resolves this conflict by committing to "dig" with his pen instead. The repetition of "Between my finger and my thumb / The squat pen rests" at the beginning and end of the poem serves to bookend this resolution, showing the speaker's acceptance of his chosen path while still honoring his heritage.

Conclusion:

In "Digging," Seamus Heaney masterfully explores the themes of heritage and identity through the use of imagery, symbolism, and structure. The poem reflects the poet's deep respect for his family's history of manual labor, while also asserting his own identity as a writer. Through his pen, Heaney continues the legacy of his ancestors in a different form, "digging" into his memories, experiences, and cultural roots to unearth the rich soil of his poetic identity. This blend of past and present, tradition and innovation, makes "Digging" a powerful meditation on the ways in which we honor our heritage while forging our own paths.

*****

SELF – PROTECTION – D.H. LAWRENCE

When science starts to be interpretive
It is more unscientific even than mysticism.

To make self-preservation and self-protection the first law of existence
Is about as scientific as making suicide the first law of existence,
And amounts to very much the same thing.

A nightingale singing at the top of his voice
Is neither hiding himself nor preserving himself nor propagating his species;
He is giving himself away in every sense of the word;
And obviously, it is the culminating point of his existence.

A tiger is striped and golden for his own glory.
He would certainly be much more invisible if he were grey-green.
And I don't suppose the ichthyosaurus sparkled like the humming-bird,

No doubt he was khaki-colored with muddy protective coloration,
So why didn't he survive?

As a matter of fact, the only creatures that seem to survive
Are those that give themselves away in flash and sparkle
And gay flicker of joyful life;
Those that go glittering abroad
With a bit of splendor.

Even mice play quite beautifully at shadows,
And some of them are brilliantly piebald.
I expect the dodo looked like a clod,
A drab and dingy bird.

About the Poet:
D.H. Lawrence (1885-1930) was an English novelist, poet, essayist, and literary critic, best known for his novels like "Sons and Lovers," "The Rainbow," "Women in Love," and "Lady Chatterley's Lover." Born in Eastwood, Nottinghamshire, Lawrence grew up in a working-class family, and his experiences in this environment deeply influenced his writing.

Lawrence's work often explores themes of human sexuality, emotional health, and the conflicts between industrial society and natural instincts. He was deeply concerned with the dehumanizing effects of modern industrialization and believed in the importance of reconnecting with nature and primal instincts. His writing reflects a keen psychological insight and a profound interest in the complexities of human relationships.

Lawrence is now celebrated as one of the most significant and influential writers of the 20th century, whose exploration of human consciousness and societal constraints paved the way for modernist literature.

Summary:
The poem "Self-Protection" by D.H. Lawrence explores the human tendency to shield oneself from emotional pain and vulnerability. Lawrence delves into the psychological and emotional barriers that individuals erect to avoid being hurt, and he examines the consequences of these defenses.

Opening Reflection: The poem begins with the speaker pondering the instinctual drive for self-protection. Lawrence suggests that this instinct is deeply ingrained in human nature, a response to the fear of pain and suffering. People often create emotional fortresses, distancing themselves from others and from experiences that might expose them to hurt. This instinct, while understandable, is not without its drawbacks.

Isolation and Loneliness: As the poem progresses, Lawrence shifts his focus to the repercussions of this protective behavior. By shielding themselves, individuals become isolated. The emotional walls they build not only keep out potential harm but also prevent genuine connections with others. This isolation leads to a profound sense of loneliness, as the person becomes trapped within their own defenses, cut off from the warmth and richness of human relationships.

Lawrence illustrates how this self-imposed isolation creates a disconnect from the world. In trying to avoid emotional pain, people may inadvertently deprive themselves of the very things that make life meaningful—love, companionship, and the shared human experience.

The Cost of Protection: In the final stanza, Lawrence reflects on the ultimate cost of self-protection. While these barriers may offer a sense of safety, they come at the expense of fully living. The fear of being hurt prevents individuals from taking risks, from opening themselves up to new experiences and emotions. The speaker questions whether this protection is worth the price, suggesting that in guarding against pain, people may miss out on the joys and beauty of life.

Conclusion: "Self-Protection" is a meditation on the balance between safety and vulnerability. Lawrence emphasizes that while it is natural to want to protect oneself from harm, doing so too rigidly can lead to a life of isolation and missed opportunities. The poem encourages readers to consider whether the fear of pain should dictate their actions or whether embracing vulnerability might lead to a richer, more fulfilling life.

Through vivid imagery and introspective language, Lawrence captures the internal struggle between the desire for security and the need for human connection. The poem ultimately suggests that the walls we build to protect ourselves might, in the end, do more harm than good.

Annotation:

1. "To make self-preservation and self-protection the first law of existence
Is about as scientific as making suicide the first law of existence,
And amounts to very much the same thing."

In these lines, D.H. Lawrence challenges the conventional notion that self-preservation and self-protection are the most fundamental instincts or laws of existence. He suggests that prioritizing these instincts above all else is as illogical and unscientific as making suicide the first law of existence.

Lawrence argues that an excessive focus on self-preservation can lead to a life of fear, restriction, and emotional death, which he equates with a form of suicide. By placing self-protection as the primary law, one may shut oneself off from meaningful experiences, connections, and growth, effectively killing the spirit or the true essence of life.

The comparison between self-preservation and suicide highlights the paradox that overly protecting oneself can lead to a stifled, unfulfilled existence. Lawrence advocates for a more balanced approach, where self-protection is not the sole guiding principle, allowing for vulnerability, openness, and the full experience of life.

2. I expect the dodo looked like a clod,
   A drab and dingy bird.

In these lines, D.H. Lawrence describes the dodo, a now-extinct bird, in a rather unflattering way. The speaker imagines the dodo as looking like "a clod," which conveys an image of something dull, heavy, and unattractive. The word "clod" often refers to a lump of earth, suggesting that the dodo was perceived as awkward and unremarkable.

The description of the dodo as "a drab and dingy bird" further emphasizes its plainness and lack of beauty. "Drab" and "dingy" both imply a dull, unexciting appearance, reinforcing the idea that the dodo was not a majestic or vibrant creature but rather a somber and unimpressive one.

One- word question and answers:
1. Question: What does the poem primarily explore?
   Answer: Self-protection
2. Question: What emotion does self-protection often lead to?
   Answer: Loneliness
3. Question: What is the instinct that drives people to build emotional barriers?
   Answer: Fear
4. Question: What does self-protection prevent people from experiencing fully?

Answer: Life

5. Question: What kind of barriers do people create to avoid emotional pain?

Answer: Emotional

6. Question: What does the poem suggest people miss out on due to self-protection?

Answer: Connection

7. Question: What is a key theme of the poem?

Answer: Vulnerability

8. Question: What is the cost of too much self-protection?

Answer: Isolation

9. Question: What is D.H. Lawrence's nationality?

Answer: English

10. Question: What does Lawrence challenge through this poem?

Answer: Security

Long Question and Answers:

1. Discuss the central theme of D.H. Lawrence's poem "Self-Protection" and how the poet conveys the consequences of emotional barriers.

The central theme of D.H. Lawrence's poem "Self-Protection" revolves around the human instinct to protect oneself from emotional pain and vulnerability. Lawrence explores how individuals, driven by the fear of being hurt, build emotional barriers to shield themselves from potential suffering. However, while these barriers may provide a sense of safety, they also lead to unintended consequences such as loneliness and isolation.

Lawrence suggests that in the pursuit of self-protection, people inadvertently cut themselves off from the richness of human experience. The poem delves into the paradox that while self-protection is meant to safeguard individuals, it also prevents them from fully engaging with life. By avoiding vulnerability, people miss out on genuine connections, love, and the beauty of shared human experiences.

The poet uses reflective language and vivid imagery to emphasize the cost of these emotional defenses. He portrays self-protection as a double-edged sword—while it guards against immediate pain, it ultimately leads to a deeper sense of loss. The poem encourages readers to question whether the safety offered by self-protection is worth the price of missing out on the joys and fullness of life.

In conclusion, Lawrence's "Self-Protection" is a poignant meditation on the balance between safety and vulnerability. The poet urges us to consider the value of embracing our fears and opening ourselves to the possibilities of life, even if it means risking emotional pain. The theme of the poem serves as a powerful reminder that true fulfilment often comes from overcoming our instinctual desire to shield ourselves from harm.

2. Examine the psychological conflict depicted in D.H. Lawrence's poem "Self-Protection" and its relevance to modern society.

D.H. Lawrence's poem "Self-Protection" delves into the psychological conflict between the desire for emotional safety and the need for genuine human connection. This internal struggle is a central theme of the poem and remains highly relevant to modern society, where the pressures of contemporary life often led individuals to prioritize self-protection over vulnerability.

The psychological conflict in the poem arises from the instinctual drive to avoid pain and suffering. Lawrence depicts how people, in an effort to protect themselves from emotional harm, erect barriers that isolate them from others. This conflict is rooted in the fear of being hurt, which leads to the construction of emotional walls. However, these protective measures come at a significant cost, as they prevent individuals from forming deep, meaningful relationships and fully engaging with life.

In modern society, this theme resonates strongly. The fast-paced, often impersonal nature of contemporary life, combined with the prevalence of social media and digital communication, can exacerbate feelings of isolation. Many people find themselves retreating into emotional shells, avoiding the risks associated with vulnerability. The poem's exploration of this conflict highlights the irony that while self-protection is intended to keep us safe, it often results in a sense of loneliness and disconnection.

Lawrence's depiction of this psychological conflict also speaks to the broader human experience. The tension between self-protection and the desire for connection is a universal struggle that transcends time and culture. In the poem, Lawrence suggests that the fear of vulnerability, while natural, ultimately limits our ability to experience the fullness of life. The poem challenges readers to confront their own fears and consider the value of embracing vulnerability as a path to true fulfilment.

The psychological conflict depicted in "Self-Protection" is a powerful reflection on the human condition, particularly in the context of modern society. Lawrence's exploration of this theme encourages readers to question the cost of emotional safety and to consider whether the barriers we build are worth the isolation they create. The poem's relevance to contemporary life underscores its enduring significance as a meditation on the complexities of human relationships and the importance of vulnerability.

***

WOMEN -ALICE WALKER

They were women then
My mama's generation
Husky of voice—stout of
Step
With fists as well as
Hands
How they battered down
Doors
And ironed
Starched white

Shirts
How they led
Armies
Headragged generals
Across mined
Fields
Booby-trapped
Ditches
To discover books
Desks
A place for us
How they knew what
we
Must know
Without knowing a page
Of it
Themselves.

About the Poet:

Alice Walker is an American novelist, poet, essayist, and activist, best known for her Pulitzer Prize-winning novel "The Colour Purple." Born on February 9, 1944, in Eatonton, Georgia, Walker grew up in the racially segregated South, an experience that deeply influenced her writing and activism. Her works often explore themes of race, gender, and social injustice, focusing on the lives and struggles of African American women.

In addition to "The Colour Purple," Walker has published numerous novels, short stories, essays, and collections of poetry. Her other notable works include "Meridian," "The Third Life of Grange Copeland," and "In Search of Our Mothers' Gardens," a collection of essays that examines the creative legacy of African American women.

Walker is also known for coining the term "womanist," which she defined as a black feminist or feminist of colour who appreciates and prefers women's culture, emotional flexibility, and strength. Her work as a writer and activist has made her a key figure in both the feminist and civil rights movements.

Through her writing, Alice Walker has given voice to the experiences of black women and highlighted the intersections of race, gender, and class. Her literary contributions have had a profound impact on American literature and continue to inspire readers and activists around the world.

Summary:

Alice Walker's poem "Women" is a powerful tribute to the resilience, strength, and determination of African American women, particularly those of previous generations who fought tirelessly to secure a better future for their children and descendants. The poem celebrates these women as warriors who, despite facing overwhelming challenges, paved the way for future generations with their unwavering courage and resolve.

Opening Lines: The poem begins by evoking an image of these women as warriors. Walker describes them as having "heads raggedy, but hands clean," which suggests that while they may have appeared disheveled or worn down by life's hardships, they maintained their dignity and purity of purpose. The juxtaposition of "raggedy heads" and "clean hands" underscores the physical and emotional toll of their struggles, yet also highlights their commitment to doing what was necessary, despite the personal cost.

Women as Warriors: Walker goes on to depict these women as strong, almost militant figures who were not afraid to fight for what they believed in. She uses language that conveys their readiness for battle, portraying them as warriors in a metaphorical sense. These women "battered down doors" and "carried armies on their backs," signifying the immense burdens they bore and the obstacles they overcame to ensure that their children had access to education and a better life.

The imagery of "battering down doors" is particularly powerful, symbolizing the breaking down of barriers—whether social, economic, or political—that stood in the way of progress. These women were not passive victims of their circumstances; they actively fought against the injustices that sought to keep them and their families oppressed.

Sacrifices for Education: One of the key themes of the poem is the importance these women placed on education. Walker notes that they "knew what we must know," emphasizing that they understood the power of knowledge and the necessity of education for future generations to rise above their conditions. Despite their own lack of formal education, they recognized that schooling was the key to empowerment and social mobility.

The poem suggests that these women's sacrifices were driven by a deep, almost instinctual understanding of what was needed to secure a better future for their children. They fought not just for themselves, but for the generations to come, ensuring that their descendants would have opportunities they never had.

Legacy and Impact: Walker's poem is both a tribute and a reminder of the legacy of these women. By referring to them as "my women," Walker personalizes the poem, connecting herself and her readers to this lineage of strength and determination. The poem serves as a call to remember and honor the sacrifices of those who came before, acknowledging the foundations they laid for future generations.

In the concluding lines, Walker emphasizes the enduring impact of these women's efforts. Their struggles were not in vain; their determination and sacrifices have borne fruit in the form of greater opportunities and freedoms for those who followed. The poem closes on a note of reverence, recognizing that the progress made by subsequent generations is built on the blood, sweat, and tears of these warrior women.

Conclusion: Alice Walker's "Women" is a powerful and moving tribute to the generations of African American women who, despite facing tremendous adversity, fought fiercely for the rights and opportunities of their children. The poem honors their strength, resilience, and foresight, celebrating their role as both protectors and pioneers. Through vivid imagery and evocative language, Walker captures the essence of their struggles and the lasting impact of their sacrifices, reminding us of the importance of acknowledging and respecting the legacy they left behind.

One-word question and answers:

1. Q: Who are the subjects of the poem?
A: Women
2. Q: What does the poem emphasize about women?
A: Strength
3. Q: What do women bear according to the poem?
A: Pain
4. Q: What do women possess despite challenges?
A: Courage
5. Q: What historical aspect is highlighted in the poem?
A: Struggle

Long question and answers:
1. Analyze the portrayal of women's strength and resilience in Alice Walker's poem "Women" and discuss how these qualities are depicted through the poem's imagery and themes.

In Alice Walker's poem "Women," the portrayal of women's strength and resilience is central to the poem's message.

Walker depicts women as figures of extraordinary endurance, whose lives are marked by both profound struggle and unyielding courage.

Imagery and Themes:

1. **Imagery of Labor and Suffering:** Walker employs vivid imagery to convey the physical and emotional labor that women endure. Phrases describing women bearing heavy burdens or enduring hardships evoke the image of their strength. For example, references to "hard work" and "bearing pain" symbolize the relentless challenges women face.

2. **Historical and Contemporary Struggles:** The poem juxtaposes historical and contemporary struggles, showing that women's resilience transcends time. By addressing past injustices, such as exploitation and marginalization, alongside present-day issues, Walker underscores the ongoing nature of women's resilience.

3. **Symbolism of Perseverance:** Walker uses symbolism to highlight women's perseverance. Women are portrayed as enduring figures who, despite facing systemic oppression, continue to thrive and contribute to society. This symbolism reinforces the theme of resilience, suggesting that women's strength is both inherent and cultivated through their experiences.

4. **Empowerment through Adversity:** The poem celebrates the empowerment that arises from overcoming adversity. Walker illustrates how women's strength is forged through their struggles, leading to a profound sense of self and identity. This empowerment is depicted as a form of victory over oppression and a testament to women's indomitable spirit.

Alice Walker's depiction of women's strength and resilience in "Women" is achieved through powerful imagery and themes that highlight their ability to endure and overcome challenges. The poem celebrates their courage and ongoing contributions to society, emphasizing the transformative power of their experiences.

2. Discuss the significance of historical context in shaping the themes of Alice Walker's "Women" and how it affects the poem's message about gender and identity.

The historical context plays a crucial role in shaping the themes of Alice Walker's "Women," profoundly influencing the poem's message about gender and identity.

1. **Legacy of Oppression:** Walker's historical context includes the legacy of slavery, segregation, and systemic racism that African American women have faced. This backdrop of historical oppression informs the poem's depiction of women's struggles. The historical context provides a lens through which the poem examines the endurance and resilience of women who have been marginalized and exploited.

2. **Cultural Heritage:** The historical context also includes the cultural heritage and traditions of African American women. Walker's reference to historical struggles is not just a recounting of past injustices but also an acknowledgment of the cultural strength and solidarity that has emerged from these experiences. The poem reflects the deep-rooted cultural identity that shapes women's resilience.

3. **Modern Challenges:** The historical context extends into contemporary issues of gender inequality and social injustice. Walker connects historical struggles with present-day challenges, illustrating that the fight for gender equality

is ongoing. This connection highlights the continuity of women's struggles and the enduring relevance of their resilience.

4. **Impact on Gender and Identity:** The historical context affects the poem's message about gender and identity by framing women's experiences within a larger narrative of struggle and empowerment. It underscores the complexities of identity shaped by both personal and collective histories. The poem suggests that women's identities are forged through their historical experiences and their responses to ongoing challenges.

The historical context is integral to understanding the themes of Alice Walker's "Women." It shapes the poem's exploration of gender and identity by providing a backdrop of historical oppression and cultural heritage that informs the portrayal of women's strength and resilience. The historical context enriches the poem's message, emphasizing the significance of women's experiences in shaping their identities and roles in society.

*****

Unit 2- Short-Stories

Jimmy Valentine – O Henry

"Jimmy Valentine" is a short story by O. Henry that revolves around a skilled safecracker named Jimmy Valentine.

The story begins with Jimmy Valentine being released from prison after serving ten months for his latest crime. He had a reputation as a skilled safe-cracker and was known for his ability to open safes without leaving a trace. After his release, Jimmy decides to go straight and lead a lawful life. He moves to a small town named Elmore, where he starts a successful shoe store and becomes a respected member of the community.

However, Jimmy's past catches up with him when Ben Price, a detective who had been pursuing him for years, tracks him down to Elmore. Price recognizes Jimmy despite his new identity and tries to arrest him. Before Price can make a move, a dramatic event unfolds that proves Jimmy's transformation and redemption.

One day, a little girl gets locked inside a newly installed bank vault in the town, and despite all efforts, no one can open it. Desperate, the girl's father seeks help, and Jimmy, realizing the seriousness of the situation, volunteers to open the vault. Using his old skills, he successfully opens the vault, saving the girl's life.

Witnessing this act of bravery and skill, Ben Price decides not to arrest Jimmy, acknowledging that he has genuinely reformed. Jimmy Valentine's act of saving the girl changes the perception of the townspeople towards him, solidifying his redemption and acceptance in his new life.

The story explores themes of redemption, the possibility of change, and the consequences of one's past actions. O. Henry's writing style combines irony with a heartfelt exploration of human nature, making "Jimmy Valentine" a classic tale of transformation and second chances.

Multiple Choice Questions:

1. Who is the protagonist of the story "Jimmy Valentine"?
a) Ben Price
b) Annabel Adams

c) Ralph D. Spencer

d) Jimmy Valentine

Answer: d) Jimmy Valentine

2. What is Jimmy Valentine's profession before he decides to change his life?

a) Banker

b) Detective

c) Safecracker

d) Policeman

Answer: c) Safecracker

3. Why does Jimmy Valentine decide to give up his criminal life?

a) He fears being caught by the police.

b) He falls in love with Annabel Adams.

c) He wants to start a new career.

d) He has no more safes to crack.

Answer: b) He falls in love with Annabel Adams.

4. Under what name does Jimmy Valentine start his new life?

a) Ben Price

b) Ralph D. Spencer

c) Mr. Adams

d) Elmore

Answer: b) Ralph D. Spencer

5. How does Ben Price react when he finally confronts Jimmy Valentine at the end of the story?

a) He arrests him immediately.

b) He shoots him.

c) He pretends not to recognize him.

d) He demands a bribe.

Answer: c) He pretends not to recognize him.

6. What event leads Jimmy Valentine to reveal his identity?

a) His engagement to Annabel.

b) A bank robbery.

c) A child being trapped in a safe.

d) A visit from his old friends.

Answer: c) A child being trapped in a safe.

7. Where does Jimmy Valentine first meet Annabel Adams?
a) At the bank.
b) In a hotel.
c) In a park.
d) At a social event.
Answer: a) At the bank.

8. What is the main theme of "Jimmy Valentine"?
a) Revenge
b) Redemption and transformation
c) Greed
d) Justice
Answer: b) Redemption and transformation

9. Which character in the story represents law and order?
a) Annabel Adams
b) Jimmy Valentine
c) Ralph D. Spencer
d) Ben Price
Answer: d) Ben Price

10. What is the significance of the title "A Retrieved Reformation"?
a) It refers to Jimmy's return to crime.
b) It symbolizes Jimmy's return to his old identity.
c) It highlights Jimmy's transformation into a better person.
d) It refers to Jimmy's reformation being undone.
Answer: c) It highlights Jimmy's transformation into a better person.

Long Answer Questions:

1. **Discuss the theme of redemption in "Jimmy Valentine" by O. Henry.**

The theme of redemption is central to O. Henry's "Jimmy Valentine." The protagonist, Jimmy Valentine, starts as a skilled and notorious safecracker. However, his life takes a transformative turn when he falls in love with Annabel Adams, the daughter of a bank owner in the small town of Elmore. This love motivates Jimmy to abandon his criminal past and adopt the persona of Ralph D. Spencer, a respectable businessman.

The narrative highlights the power of love and human connection to inspire personal change. Jimmy's decision to reform is not superficial; he genuinely intends to leave his criminal activities behind, evidenced by his determination to live an honest life and even consider marriage. His redemption is tested when a child is accidentally locked in a bank vault, and Jimmy must use his criminal skills to save her. Despite revealing his true identity, Jimmy is granted a second chance by Ben Price, the detective who has been pursuing him. Price's decision to let Jimmy go is a recognition of the sincerity of his transformation, affirming the theme that genuine redemption is possible and should be rewarded.

O. Henry uses irony effectively, as the same skills that made Jimmy a criminal ultimately enable his redemption. The story suggests that redemption is not just about changing behavior but about the willingness to act selflessly for the sake of others. Jimmy's reformation is complete when he prioritizes the child's life over his own freedom, proving that he has truly changed.

2. Analyze the character of Jimmy Valentine and his transformation throughout the story.

Jimmy Valentine is a complex character who undergoes significant transformation in O. Henry's "Jimmy Valentine." At the beginning of the story, Jimmy is portrayed as a charming and skilled safecracker, confident in his abilities and unrepentant about his criminal lifestyle. His easy escape from prison and immediate return to crime demonstrate his expertise and the thrill he finds in his illegal activities.

However, Jimmy's character begins to change when he arrives in the small town of Elmore and meets Annabel Adams. His attraction to her is profound enough to inspire him to reconsider his life choices. The sincerity of his feelings is evident in his decision to adopt a new identity, Ralph D. Spencer, and establish a legitimate business. This transformation is not just about changing his name but about changing his entire way of life, indicating a deep internal shift.

The climax of Jimmy's transformation occurs when a child is accidentally locked in a bank vault, and he is faced with a moral dilemma. By choosing to reveal his criminal past to save the child, Jimmy demonstrates that his transformation is genuine. He sacrifices his new identity and the life he has built for the sake of another, showing that he has truly become a better person.

The final encounter with Ben Price, the detective who has been tracking him, solidifies Jimmy's transformation. Price's decision to let him go suggests that Jimmy has earned his redemption, and his past should not define his future. Jimmy Valentine's character arc from a hardened criminal to a redeemed man highlights the story's message about the potential for personal change and the power of love and selflessness.

3. Explain the significance of Ben Price's role in the story. How does his character contribute to the resolution of the plot?

Ben Price plays a crucial role in "Jimmy Valentine," serving as both an antagonist and a moral compass within the story. As a detective, Price represents law and order, tirelessly pursuing Jimmy Valentine after his release from prison and subsequent return to safecracking. His character is characterized by his dedication and intelligence, making him a formidable opponent for Jimmy.

Price's significance lies in his role as the arbiter of justice. Throughout the story, he is portrayed as a determined detective who understands Jimmy's methods and is committed to capturing him. However, his role shifts dramatically at the story's climax. When Price arrives in Elmore to arrest Jimmy, he witnesses an extraordinary act of selflessness: Jimmy uses his safecracking skills to rescue a child locked in a bank vault, fully aware that this act will reveal his true identity and lead to his arrest.

This act of heroism forces Price to reconsider his perception of Jimmy. The moment serves as a moral turning point in the story. Price sees that Jimmy has genuinely reformed and is no longer the man he once pursued. By pretending not to recognize Jimmy and allowing him to continue his life as Ralph D. Spencer, Price becomes an instrument of grace rather than strict justice.

Ben Price's decision to let Jimmy go underscores the theme of redemption and suggests that true justice sometimes involves mercy. His character contributes to the resolution by acknowledging the profound change in Jimmy, allowing the story to end on a hopeful note. Price's actions highlight the possibility of redemption and the idea that people are capable of genuine transformation.

***

The Best Investment I Ever Made – A .J. Cronin

"The Best Investment I Ever Made" is a short story by A.J. Cronin that explores themes of compassion, redemption, and the impact of small acts of kindness.

Setting and Introduction

The story begins with the narrator, Dr. A.J. Cronin himself, who is aboard a ship on a voyage from the United States to England. He observes a fellow passenger, Mr.

John Singleton, who seems to be of a modest background but carries himself with dignity and calmness. Dr. Cronin finds himself inexplicably drawn to this man, sensing that there is something familiar about him.

The Meeting

One evening, during the voyage, Mr. Singleton approaches Dr. Cronin and introduces himself. He reminds Dr. Cronin of an incident that had occurred many years ago. Initially, Cronin does not remember him, but as Singleton recounts his story, the memory begins to resurface.

Flashback: The Troubled Youth

The story shifts into a flashback where we learn about John Singleton's troubled past. Many years earlier, Singleton was a young man in London, caught in the throes of despair and depression due to a series of unfortunate events. He had lost his job, fallen into bad company, and eventually, in a moment of weakness, he stole money from his employer and lost it all in gambling. Overwhelmed by guilt and hopelessness, Singleton attempted suicide.

Dr. Cronin's Intervention

At this point in the story, Dr. Cronin enters as a young doctor who was called to attend to Singleton after his suicide attempt. Recognizing the young man's desperate state, Cronin decides to help him. Instead of reporting him to the police, Dr. Cronin offers him guidance and a second chance. He pays off Singleton's debt with his own money, which he considers his best investment, and gives him a fresh start. Singleton is deeply moved by this act of kindness and promises to turn his life around.

Transformation and Redemption

Singleton takes Dr. Cronin's words to heart and completely reforms his life. He becomes a devoted social worker, dedicating his life to helping troubled youth and those in need, much like he once was. His organization, which he runs with his wife, has helped countless young people find their way back to a meaningful life. Singleton's transformation is not just about personal redemption; it has had a ripple effect, impacting the lives of many others.

Conclusion

The story concludes with Singleton expressing his deep gratitude to Dr. Cronin for saving his life and giving him a chance to make something of himself. Cronin reflects on how his small act of kindness, which he initially saw as a financial sacrifice, turned out to be the best investment he ever made, as it resulted in the saving of not just one life, but many.

Themes and Message

"The Best Investment I Ever Made" highlights the power of compassion and the profound impact that one person's kindness can have on another's life. It underscores the idea that sometimes the most valuable investments are not financial but are those made in people, offering them hope and a second chance when they need it most. The story is a testament to the transformative power of generosity and the importance of believing in the potential for change in others.

Multiple Choice Questions:

1. What is the profession of the narrator in "The Best Investment I Ever Made"?

a) Lawyer

b) Doctor

c) Teacher

d) Engineer

Answer: b) Doctor

2. What was the young man's name whom the narrator helped?

a) John

b) Michael

c) John Syme

d) Mr. Rees

Answer: c) John Syme

3. How did the narrator first meet John Syme?

a) At a hospital

b) During a suicide attempt

c) At a social event

d) On a train

Answer: b) During a suicide attempt

4. Why was John Syme attempting suicide?

a) He was suffering from a terminal illness.

b) He had lost his job.

c) He was in debt and felt hopeless.

d) He had a failed relationship.

Answer: c) He was in debt and felt hopeless.

5. What did the narrator do to help John Syme?

a) He gave him a job.

b) He provided him with money.

c) He offered him free medical treatment.

d) He gave him counseling and legal help.

Answer: d) He gave him counseling and legal help.

6. How did John Syme's life change after receiving help from the narrator?

a) He became a successful businessman.

b) He became a social worker and dedicated his life to helping others.

c) He moved to another country.

d) He went back to his previous job.

Answer: b) He became a social worker and dedicated his life to helping others.

7. What does the title "The Best Investment I Ever Made" refer to?

a) The money the narrator invested in stocks.

b) The time and effort the narrator invested in helping John Syme.

c) The narrator's investment in property.

d) The narrator's career choice.

Answer: b) The time and effort the narrator invested in helping John Syme.

8. What emotion does the narrator feel towards John Syme at the end of the story?

a) Regret

b) Pride

c) Anger

d) Indifference

Answer: b) Pride

9. What lesson does the narrator learn from his experience with John Syme?

a) That investing in stocks is the best way to secure a future.

b) That small acts of kindness can have a lasting impact on someone's life.

c) That it's important to be cautious with money.

d) That people cannot change their fate.

Answer: b) That small acts of kindness can have a lasting impact on someone's life.

10. What is the setting of the story's climax?
 a) In the narrator's office
 b) On a ship
 c) In a courtroom
 d) At a charity event
Answer: b) On a ship

Long Answer Questions:

1. Discuss the significance of the title "The Best Investment I Ever Made" in the context of the story.

The title "The Best Investment I Ever Made" holds deep significance in A.J. Cronin's story, both literally and metaphorically. Typically, when we think of an investment, we imagine a financial or material commitment intended to yield future benefits. However, in this story, the "investment" refers to the time, compassion, and moral support the narrator, Dr. Cronin, provided to a troubled young man named John Syme.

Dr. Cronin's investment was not monetary but emotional and psychological. He helped John during a moment of extreme despair, when the young man attempted suicide due to overwhelming guilt and financial distress. Dr. Cronin, along with a judge and a police officer, intervened not only to save John's life but also to set him on a path to redemption by offering him counseling and legal assistance.

This investment pays off in a way that Dr. Cronin had not anticipated. Years later, on a voyage to the United States, Dr. Cronin encounters John Syme again, now a successful social worker who has dedicated his life to helping troubled boys. John's transformation from a suicidal young man to a compassionate and effective social worker demonstrates the profound impact of Dr. Cronin's investment. The narrator reflects on how this small act of kindness had a ripple effect, helping not just John but many others through his subsequent work.

The title suggests that the most valuable investments are those made in people, not in financial terms, but in terms of time, care, and support. Dr. Cronin realizes that the return on this investment—seeing John thrive and contribute positively to society—is far greater than any material gain he could have received. This realization underlines the theme of the story: the power of human kindness and the long-lasting impact it can have on someone's life.

2. Analyze the character of John Syme and his transformation in the story "The Best Investment I Ever Made."

John Syme is a pivotal character in "The Best Investment I Ever Made," whose journey from despair to redemption is central to the story's theme. Initially, John is depicted as a young man in a dire situation. Overwhelmed by debt and feeling utterly hopeless, he attempts to take his own life. This action portrays him as someone who has reached the end of his tether, unable to see a way out of his problems. He is a representation of the vulnerability and desperation that can lead people to make tragic decisions.

However, John Syme's character undergoes a significant transformation, thanks to the intervention of Dr. Cronin and other compassionate individuals. The help he receives is not just legal or financial but also moral and psychological. This support helps him regain his self-worth and gives him a second chance at life.

John's transformation is most evident in his career choice following this intervention. He becomes a social worker, dedicating his life to helping troubled and disadvantaged boys. This career path reflects his deep sense of gratitude and his desire to give back to society. He turns his own experience of despair into a driving force for good, using his understanding of suffering to aid others in similar situations.

The character of John Syme illustrates the idea that people can change drastically when given support and a second chance. His transformation from a desperate, suicidal young man to a successful, empathetic social worker highlights the story's central theme of redemption and the lasting impact that kindness and compassion can have on a person's life.

Furthermore, John's transformation serves as a testament to the idea that even those who have hit rock bottom can rise again and make a positive impact on the world. His character arc also underscores the importance of social support systems and the role of empathy in helping individuals rebuild their lives.

***

The Refugee – K .A .Abbas

"The Refugee" by K.A. Abbas is a poignant short story that explores the themes of displacement, identity, and the human condition against the backdrop of the partition of India in 1947. The story delves into the lives of those who were uprooted from their homes and forced to start anew in unfamiliar places.

Setting and Introduction

The story is set in India during the time of the partition, a period marked by widespread communal violence and the mass migration of millions of people across newly drawn borders. The story revolves around the central character, Gulam Ali, an elderly man who becomes a refugee due to the partition. He is forced to leave his home in Pakistan and migrate to India.

Arrival at the Refugee Camp

Gulam Ali arrives at a refugee camp in India, carrying with him nothing but a few belongings and a profound sense of loss. The camp is overcrowded and filled with people who share similar stories of displacement and suffering. Despite the dire conditions, Gulam Ali maintains a dignified demeanor, trying to make the best of the situation.

Gulam Ali's Struggles

At the camp, Gulam Ali struggles to adjust to his new reality. He is haunted by memories of his past life in Pakistan, where he had lived peacefully and with pride. The transition from being a respected member of his community to a refugee in a foreign land is a bitter pill to swallow. He finds it difficult to accept his new identity as a "refugee," which strips him of his former dignity and self-respect.

The Loss of Identity

The story emphasizes the loss of identity experienced by refugees like Gulam Ali. In the camp, he is no longer recognized as the person he once was; he is now just one among many nameless, faceless individuals who have lost everything. This loss of identity is compounded by the fact that he is now dependent on others for survival, a stark contrast to his previous life of independence.

Encounter with the Younger Generation

Gulam Ali's struggles are highlighted further when he interacts with the younger generation in the camp. The youth, having been born in the refugee camp or displaced at a very young age, have no memory of the life that was lost. They have adapted to the harsh conditions and are focused on survival, often indifferent to the pain and nostalgia that the older generation like Gulam Ali carries with them. This generational gap adds to Gulam Ali's sense of isolation and despair.

Conclusion: A Life of Resilience

Despite the overwhelming challenges, Gulam Ali displays resilience. He tries to hold onto his memories and his sense of self, even in the face of adversity. The story does not offer a conventional resolution but rather leaves the reader with a deep sense of the enduring pain and hardship faced by refugees. Gulam Ali's struggle to maintain his dignity and identity in the midst of his suffering is a powerful commentary on the human cost of displacement and the partition.

Themes and Message

"The Refugee" by K.A. Abbas is a moving narrative that sheds light on the psychological and emotional toll of being a refugee. The story captures the profound sense of loss that comes with being uprooted from one's homeland and the challenges of rebuilding one's life in a foreign land. It also highlights the generational differences in coping with displacement, where the older generation is burdened with memories of the past, while the younger generation is focused on the present and future.

The story is a powerful reminder of the enduring impact of the partition on individuals and communities, and it underscores the resilience of the human spirit in the face of unimaginable hardship.

Multiple Choice Questions:

1. What is the central theme of "The Refugee" by K.A. Abbas?

A) Political corruption
B) Social inequality
C) The plight of refugees and human compassion
D) Economic disparity
Answer: C) The plight of refugees and human compassion
2. What is the name of the main character in "The Refugee"?
A) Mr. Gupta
B) Mr. Sharma
C) Mr. Khan
D) Mr. Ahmed
Answer: C) Mr. Khan
3. What does Mr. Khan, the refugee, seek from the narrator in the story?
A) Money
B) Shelter
C) Employment
D) Legal assistance
Answer: B) Shelter
4. How does the narrator initially respond to Mr. Khan's request for help?
A) With immediate generosity
B) With suspicion and reluctance
C) With indifference
D) With enthusiasm
Answer: B) With suspicion and reluctance

5. What significant action does the narrator take towards the end of the story?
A) Rejects Mr. Khan's request
B) Provides Mr. Khan with a job
C) Offers Mr. Khan a place to stay
D) Informs Mr. Khan about refugee camps
Answer: C) Offers Mr. Khan a place to stay

6. Which aspect of human nature does "The Refugee" highlight through its characters?
A) Greed
B) Prejudice
C) Empathy
D) Arrogance
Answer: C) Empathy
7. In the story, what does the narrator's change of heart represent?
A) His financial stability
B) His growing awareness of social issues
C) His personal gain
D) His dissatisfaction with life
Answer: B) His growing awareness of social issues

Long Answer Questions:

1. Discuss the portrayal of human compassion and social responsibility in "The Refugee." How does the story reflect these themes through its characters and events?

In "The Refugee," K.A. Abbas effectively portrays human compassion and social responsibility through the interactions between the main character, Mr. Khan, and the narrator. Mr. Khan, a refugee, represents the plight of many displaced individuals seeking refuge and assistance. The narrator's initial reaction is one of suspicion and reluctance, reflecting a common societal attitude towards refugees. However, as the story progresses, the narrator's transformation showcases a shift from indifference to empathy. This change is catalyzed by Mr. Khan's plight and the narrator's realization of the broader social responsibilities.

The narrator's eventual decision to offer Mr. Khan shelter reflects a deeper understanding of social responsibility. This act of kindness illustrates that true compassion involves recognizing and addressing the needs of others, particularly those who are vulnerable and displaced. The story highlights that human compassion is not merely about feeling pity but also about taking concrete actions to alleviate suffering. By the end of the story, the narrator embodies the ideal of social responsibility, showing that empathy can lead to positive change and support for those in dire circumstances.

2. Evaluate the character development of the narrator in "The Refugee." How does his attitude towards Mr. Khan evolve throughout the story?

The narrator in "The Refugee" undergoes significant character development, particularly in his attitude towards Mr. Khan. At the beginning of the story, the narrator is characterized by his indifference and suspicion. He views Mr. Khan's request for help with skepticism, reflecting a common societal attitude towards refugees and their claims.

As the narrative unfolds, the narrator's interactions with Mr. Khan and the refugee's earnest plea for assistance prompt a shift in his perspective. The narrator begins to empathize with Mr. Khan's situation, recognizing the gravity of his plight and the broader implications of his request. This change is driven by a growing awareness of the human suffering that Mr. Khan represents and a realization of the narrator's own social responsibility.

By the end of the story, the narrator's character arc is completed when he decides to offer Mr. Khan a place to stay. This act signifies a transformation from indifference to empathy and highlights the narrator's newfound commitment to addressing the needs of those less fortunate. The development of the narrator's character is central to the story's theme of compassion and social responsibility, illustrating how personal growth can lead to positive societal impact.

3. Explore the use of symbolism in "The Refugee." How does Abbas use symbols to enhance the themes of the story?

K.A. Abbas employs various symbols in "The Refugee" to enhance the story's themes of compassion and social responsibility. One of the primary symbols is the narrator's home, which initially represents comfort, security, and detachment from the broader social issues. This home, as a symbol of privilege, contrasts with Mr. Khan's dire situation, highlighting the disparity between the two characters.

Mr. Khan himself symbolizes the broader refugee crisis and the human suffering associated with displacement. His plight serves as a poignant reminder of the vulnerability of refugees and the need for societal empathy and support. His humble appearance and desperate plea symbolize the larger issues faced by many refugees.

As the story progresses, the narrator's decision to offer Mr. Khan shelter transforms the home from a symbol of isolation to one of refuge and compassion. This shift reflects the narrator's personal growth and the story's underlying message about the importance of empathy and social responsibility. Through these symbols, Abbas deepens the reader's understanding of the themes and the impact of individual actions on addressing social issues.

***

Unit 3- Essays
On Superstitions by A. G. Gardiner

A.G. Gardiner's essay "On Superstitions" is a witty and insightful exploration of the nature and persistence of superstitious beliefs in society. Gardiner examines how superstitions, though often dismissed as irrational or outdated, continue to exert a strong influence on people's lives, even among those who consider themselves modern and enlightened.

The essay begins with Gardiner reflecting on the universal presence of superstitions across different cultures and societies. He notes that superstitions have a long history, deeply rooted in human psychology. Despite advancements in science and education, people still cling to these irrational beliefs, which can range from simple practices like avoiding walking under a ladder to more complex rituals meant to ward off bad luck.

Gardiner argues that superstitions persist because they offer a sense of control in an unpredictable world. People often turn to superstitious practices in moments of uncertainty, fear, or anxiety, seeking comfort in the idea that they can influence their fate. This is particularly true in situations where rational explanations or solutions are lacking.

The essay also touches on the irony of how even those who reject superstitions on an intellectual level may still find themselves subconsciously influenced by them. Gardiner humorously describes how otherwise rational individuals might hesitate before doing something considered unlucky, such as spilling salt or breaking a mirror, even if they don't truly believe in the associated consequences.

Gardiner further explores the social aspect of superstitions, observing how they are often passed down through generations and reinforced by cultural traditions. He notes that some superstitions have become so ingrained in daily life that people follow them almost automatically, without questioning their origins or validity.

In his conclusion, Gardiner acknowledges that while superstitions are irrational, they are also a part of the human experience. He suggests that rather than attempting to eradicate them entirely, it might be more realistic to accept them as an enduring aspect of human nature. However, he also encourages readers to be aware of the potential harm that can arise when superstitions are taken too seriously or used to justify harmful actions.

Analysis: Gardiner's essay is a blend of humor, insight, and reflection, making it an engaging read that encourages readers to examine their own beliefs and behaviors. He skillfully balances criticism of superstitions with an understanding of their psychological and cultural significance, offering a nuanced perspective on why these beliefs persist.

Through his writing, Gardiner invites readers to recognize the irrationality of superstitions while also acknowledging their comfort and familiarity. His essay ultimately serves as a reminder of the complexities of human nature and the ways in which tradition and belief can shape our lives, even in a modern, rational world.

Multiple Choice Questions:

1. What is the primary reason Gardiner gives for the persistence of superstitions in modern society?
a) Lack of education
b) Psychological comfort and a sense of control
c) Influence of media
d) Scientific ignorance
Answer: b) Psychological comfort and a sense of control

2. Which of the following does Gardiner use to illustrate the absurdity of superstitions?
a) Historical events
b) Scientific experiments
c) Everyday examples and situations
d) Religious texts
Answer: c) Everyday examples and situations
3. According to Gardiner, superstitions are often passed down through:
a) Personal experiences
b) Cultural traditions and social practices
c) Formal education
d) Government regulations
Answer: b) Cultural traditions and social practices

4. Gardiner suggests that the belief in superstitions provides people with:
a) A logical explanation for events
b) A means to control others
c) Comfort in the face of uncertainty
d) A way to demonstrate intelligence
Answer: c) Comfort in the face of uncertainty
5. How does Gardiner approach the topic of superstitions in his essay?
a) With strict criticism and rejection
b) With a balanced view, acknowledging their place in human nature
c) By fully endorsing them
d) By ignoring their existence
Answer: b) With a balanced view, acknowledging their place in human nature
6. Gardiner uses irony in his essay to show:
a) How superstitions are logically sound
b) The contradiction between people's beliefs and their actions
c) The scientific basis of superstitions
d) The importance of holding onto superstitions
Answer: b) The contradiction between people's beliefs and their actions
7. Which of the following best describes Gardiner's view on the complete eradication of superstitions?
a) It is essential for progress
b) It is possible with enough education
c) It might be unrealistic due to their deep roots in human nature
d) It should be enforced by law
Answer: c) It might be unrealistic due to their deep roots in human nature
8. What does Gardiner suggest about people who claim not to believe in superstitions?
a) They are completely free from any superstitious behavior
b) They may still unconsciously follow superstitious practices
c) They are the most rational individuals in society
d) They are not influenced by cultural traditions

Answer: b) They may still unconsciously follow superstitious practices

9. Gardiner believes that superstitions have persisted over time primarily because:

a) They are scientifically proven

b) They provide psychological and emotional comfort

c) They are legally enforced

d) They are taught in schools

Answer: b) They provide psychological and emotional comfort

10. What tone does Gardiner use in his essay "On Superstitions"?

a) Serious and somber

b) Humorous and reflective

c) Aggressive and critical

d) Indifferent and detached

Answer: b) Humorous and reflective

Long Answer Questions:

1. Discuss the psychological factors that contribute to the persistence of superstitions, as explained by A.G. Gardiner in his essay "On Superstitions." How do these factors influence people's behaviour?

Gardiner identifies several psychological factors that contribute to the persistence of superstitions. Firstly, he notes that superstitions provide a sense of control in an uncertain world. People often turn to superstitious practices when they face situations where rational explanations or solutions are insufficient. For instance, someone might carry a lucky charm before a difficult exam to feel more confident, even if they know it has no real effect. This psychological comfort can make superstitions deeply ingrained in behaviour.

Secondly, Gardiner highlights the role of fear and anxiety. Superstitions often arise from a fear of the unknown or from a desire to avoid bad luck. The fear of potential negative outcomes can compel individuals to adhere to superstitious practices, even if they don't fully believe in them. For example, avoiding walking under a ladder might be driven by an underlying anxiety about tempting fate.

Lastly, the repetition of superstitions through cultural and social practices reinforces these beliefs, making them part of a collective consciousness. Even those who consider themselves rational may find it hard to break free from these habits due to their deep psychological roots.

2. Examine the cultural significance of superstitions as portrayed by A.G. Gardiner. How do cultural traditions contribute to the maintenance and transmission of superstitious beliefs?

Gardiner explores how cultural traditions play a crucial role in maintaining and transmitting superstitions. He observes that many superstitions are deeply embedded in cultural practices, passed down through generations almost unconsciously. For example, certain rituals or taboos may be followed during weddings, funerals, or other significant life events without question.

These traditions are often linked to a community's identity, making them difficult to challenge or discard. Gardiner notes that people might adhere to superstitions not because they believe in them, but because they are a part of their cultural heritage. This social dimension ensures that superstitions remain a collective experience, reinforced by family, community, and societal norms.

Gardiner suggests that superstitions are often accepted because they are intertwined with the values and beliefs of a culture. Challenging these superstitions might be seen as challenging the culture itself, leading to their persistence even in the face of modern rationality.

3. In "On Superstitions," A.G. Gardiner explores the contrast between rationality and irrationality in human behavior. Discuss how he presents this contrast and its implications for understanding human nature.

Gardiner presents the contrast between rationality and irrationality as a central theme in his essay. He illustrates how, despite the progress of science and education, superstitions continue to thrive, revealing the irrational side of human nature. This contrast is evident in the way people, who are otherwise logical and educated, still adhere to superstitious practices.

Gardiner suggests that this irrationality is not entirely negative; it is a part of what makes us human. He implies that the coexistence of rationality and irrationality reflects the complexity of human psychology. People may understand that superstitions lack a scientific basis, but they still find comfort in them because they address emotional and psychological needs that logic cannot.

This duality in human nature has broader implications for understanding behavior. Gardiner's essay suggests that even in a modern, rational society, emotions, fears, and traditions will always play a significant role in shaping how we act. The persistence of superstitions serves as a reminder that human behavior is not solely governed by logic and reason, but also by deeper, often subconscious forces.

***

The Light Has Gone Out – Jawaharlal Nehru

"The Light Has Gone Out" is a poignant speech delivered by Jawaharlal Nehru, India's first Prime Minister, on the death of Mahatma Gandhi on January 30, 1948. Nehru's speech reflects the profound impact Gandhi had on India and the world, and it captures the sense of loss felt by the nation.

Summary: Opening Sentiments: Nehru begins his speech with a somber tone, acknowledging the deep grief and shock that has overtaken the nation following Gandhi's assassination. He uses the metaphor of light to symbolize Gandhi's life and contributions, stating that the light has gone out of our lives. This metaphor conveys the profound sense of loss and the darkness that now envelops India in the wake of Gandhi's death.

Tribute to Gandhi: Nehru highlights Gandhi's unparalleled influence and contributions to the Indian freedom struggle. He describes Gandhi as a guiding force who led the country through its darkest times with his ideals of non-violence, truth, and justice. Gandhi's leadership, he argues, was not just about political strategies but also about moral and spiritual guidance. His commitment to the principles of non-violence (ahimsa) and his ability to inspire millions made him a beacon of hope and strength.

Impact on the Nation: Nehru reflects on the personal and collective grief of the Indian people. He acknowledges that Gandhi's death is not only a loss of a leader but also of a beloved father figure who had become synonymous with the struggle for independence and the vision of a free and united India. Nehru emphasizes that Gandhi's death leaves a void that cannot be filled, underscoring the emotional and psychological impact on the nation.

Call to Action: In the face of this tremendous loss, Nehru calls upon the people of India to honour Gandhi's legacy by continuing his work and adhering to his principles. He urges the nation to stay united and to strive for the ideals Gandhi championed. Nehru emphasizes that the best way to commemorate Gandhi's life is to continue working towards the goals he had set for India—peace, justice, and social harmony

Reflection on Gandhi's Vision: Nehru reflects on Gandhi's vision for India and the world. He acknowledges that Gandhi's teachings extended beyond Indian borders and had a universal appeal. Gandhi's philosophy of non-violence and his quest for justice and equality had resonated globally. Nehru asserts that while Gandhi may have left the physical world, his ideals and teachings would continue to guide and inspire future generations.

Conclusion: Nehru concludes his speech with a call for resolve and perseverance. He stresses that although the nation has lost a great leader, the spirit of Gandhi's teachings should continue to live on in the hearts and actions of the Indian people. He expresses hope that the values Gandhi stood for will continue to light the way forward, even in his absence.

Overall, Nehru's speech is a moving tribute to Mahatma Gandhi, capturing both the profound sense of loss felt by the nation and the enduring impact of Gandhi's legacy. It serves as a reminder of the need to uphold the principles of truth, non-violence, and justice, which Gandhi had so passionately advocated throughout his life.

Multiple Choice Questions:
1. What metaphor does Nehru use to describe the impact of Gandhi's death?
A) The star has dimmed
B) The sun has set
C) The light has gone out
D) The moon has faded
Answer: C) The light has gone out
2. In his speech, how does Nehru characterize Gandhi's role in the Indian freedom struggle?
A) As a mere politician
B) As a military leader
C) As a guiding force and moral leader
D) As an economic reformer
Answer: C) As a guiding force and moral leader
3. What does Nehru urge the Indian people to do in the face of Gandhi's death?
A) Mourn in silence
B) Disband political activities
C) Continue Gandhi's work and uphold his principles
D) Seek revenge for his assassination
Answer: C) Continue Gandhi's work and uphold his principles

4. According to Nehru, what was one of Gandhi's key contributions beyond India?
A) Promoting military strength
B) Advocating for global economic reforms
C) Spreading the philosophy of non-violence and justice worldwide
D) Leading scientific advancements
Answer: C) Spreading the philosophy of non-violence and justice worldwide
5. How does Nehru describe the impact of Gandhi's death on the Indian nation?
A) It was a minor event with little impact
B) It was a loss that left a void and caused immense grief
C) It brought about immediate political change
D) It led to economic hardships
Answer: B) It was a loss that left a void and caused immense grief
6. What was Nehru's main message about Gandhi's teachings in his speech?
A) They should be forgotten
B) They should be used for political gain
C) They should continue to inspire and guide future generations
D) They are no longer relevant
Answer: C) They should continue to inspire and guide future generations

7. How does Nehru suggest that Gandhi's legacy should be honoured?
A) By holding memorial services
B) By continuing to work towards the goals Gandhi set for India
C) By establishing monuments in his name
D) By writing about his life in books
Answer: B) By continuing to work towards the goals Gandhi set for India
8. What does Nehru reflect upon regarding Gandhi's influence on the world?
A) Gandhi's influence was limited to India
B) Gandhi's teachings were irrelevant to the global community

C) Gandhi's ideals had a universal appeal and resonated globally
D) Gandhi was primarily a national figure without global impact
Answer: C) Gandhi's ideals had a universal appeal and resonated globally
9. What emotional tone is prevalent throughout Nehru's speech?
A) Joyful and celebratory
B) Indifferent and detached
C) Somber and reflective
D) Angry and confrontational
Answer: C) Somber and reflective
10. What key value does Nehru emphasize as essential to carry forward in Gandhi's absence?
A) Wealth accumulation
B) Military strength
C) Non-violence and justice
D) Technological progress
Answer: C) Non-violence and justice

Long Answers Questions:

1. Discuss the historical context and significance of Jawaharlal Nehru's speech "The Light Has Gone Out."

Jawaharlal Nehru delivered the speech "The Light Has Gone Out" on January 30, 1948, following the assassination of Mahatma Gandhi. This speech holds profound historical significance as it mourns the loss of Gandhi, not just as a leader but as the moral compass of the Indian independence movement. Nehru's words reflected the shock and grief of a nation that revered Gandhi as the Father of the Nation. The speech highlighted Gandhi's immense contributions to India's struggle for freedom, his principles of non-violence, and his vision for a united and independent India. It also underscored the immediate impact of Gandhi's absence on the nation's spirit and the challenges ahead in maintaining his ideals amidst communal tensions and political uncertainties. Nehru's speech resonated deeply with the Indian public and the international community, emphasizing Gandhi's universal influence and the monumental loss felt across the world.

2. Analyze the rhetorical devices used by Jawaharlal Nehru in his speech "The Light Has Gone Out."

Jawaharlal Nehru's speech "The Light Has Gone Out" is a masterful example of rhetoric, employing various devices to convey profound grief and evoke national unity:

- Pathos: Nehru appeals to the emotions of the audience, expressing deep sorrow and mourning over the loss of Mahatma Gandhi, using poignant language to evoke empathy and solidarity.
- Anaphora: The repetition of the phrase "The light has gone out" throughout the speech emphasizes the magnitude of Gandhi's absence and its impact on the nation.
- Metaphor: Nehru uses metaphors like "a flame has been extinguished" to symbolize Gandhi's life and ideals, portraying him as a guiding light in India's struggle for freedom.
- Antithesis: Nehru contrasts the darkness caused by Gandhi's death with the brightness of his life and principles, highlighting the stark contrast between loss and the enduring legacy of non-violence and unity.
- Appeal to ethos: As a close associate of Gandhi and the first Prime Minister of independent India, Nehru's authority and personal connection to the subject lend credibility and emotional depth to his words.

These rhetorical devices not only enhance the emotional impact of Nehru's speech but also reinforce Gandhi's legacy and the enduring relevance of his principles in India's post-independence era.

***

Town by the Sea- Amitav Ghosh

"Town by the Sea" by Amitav Ghosh is a reflective and poignant essay that delves into the aftermath of the 2004 Indian Ocean tsunami. The essay is part of Ghosh's book "The Great Derangement: Climate Change and the Unthinkable" and it captures his personal experience of visiting the town of Galle in Sri Lanka, which was devastated by the tsunami.

Summary:

The essay begins with Ghosh recounting his relationship with the town of Galle, a place he had visited several times before the tsunami struck. Ghosh describes Galle as a serene and picturesque town by the sea, with its historic fort, vibrant community, and stunning coastline. However, the tranquillity of the town was shattered on December 26, 2004, when the tsunami ravaged the Indian Ocean region, leaving death and destruction in its wake.

Ghosh vividly describes the devastation caused by the tsunami, painting a picture of the immense scale of the disaster. He recounts the harrowing stories of survivors, many of whom lost their loved ones, homes, and livelihoods in a matter of minutes. The essay captures the chaos, confusion, and heartbreak that followed the disaster, as well as the overwhelming sense of loss experienced by the community.

As Ghosh walks through the ruins of Galle, he reflects on the fragility of human life and the vulnerability of coastal communities to natural disasters. He contrasts the beauty of the town before the tsunami with the desolation he witnesses in its aftermath. The essay is also a meditation on memory, loss, and the passage of time. Ghosh reflects on how the town he once knew has been irrevocably changed, both physically and in the collective memory of its inhabitants.

Ghosh also explores the broader implications of the tsunami, touching on themes of environmental change and human resilience. He discusses the unpredictable nature of such disasters and the challenges faced by those trying to rebuild their lives in the wake of such a calamity. The essay raises important questions about humanity's relationship with nature and the need for greater awareness and preparedness in the face of environmental threats.

"Town by the Sea" is a powerful and evocative piece that captures the profound impact of the 2004 tsunami on a small coastal town in Sri Lanka. Through his personal reflections and observations, Ghosh offers a poignant commentary on loss, memory, and the enduring human spirit in the face of overwhelming tragedy.

Multiple Choice Questions:

1. What is the central theme of Amitav Ghosh's essay "Town by the Sea"?
a) Urbanization
b) Cultural heritage
c) Natural disaster and its aftermath
d) Economic development
Answer: c) Natural disaster and its aftermath
2. Which natural disaster is the focus of "Town by the Sea"?
a) Earthquake
b) Tsunami
c) Hurricane
d) Flood
Answer: b) Tsunami
3. Where is the town that Ghosh visits in "Town by the Sea" located?
a) India
b) Thailand
c) Sri Lanka
d) Indonesia

Answer: c) Sri Lanka

4. What is the name of the town that Ghosh describes in the essay?

a) Colombo

b) Galle

c) Kandy

d) Trincomalee

Answer: b) Galle

5.In "Town by the Sea," how does Ghosh describe the town before the tsunami?

a) A bustling metropolis

b) A serene and picturesque town

c) A rundown and neglected area

d) A rapidly developing city

Answer: b) A serene and picturesque town

6.What does Ghosh reflect on as he walks through the ruins of the town?

a) The economic potential of the area

b) The beauty of the town before the disaster

c) The political history of the region

d) The cultural diversity of the inhabitants

Answer: b) The beauty of the town before the disaster

7. Which of the following is NOT a theme explored in "Town by the Sea"?

a) The unpredictability of natural disasters

b) The impact of colonialism

c) Human resilience

d) The fragility of life

Answer: b) The impact of colonialism

8.What broader topic does Ghosh touch upon in the essay?

a) Climate change and environmental threats

b) Technological advancements

c) Political instability

d) Globalization

Answer: a) Climate change and environmental threats

9.How does Ghosh describe the collective memory of the town's inhabitants after the tsunami?
a) Unchanged and resilient
b) Full of hope and optimism
c) Irrevocably altered by the disaster
d) Focused solely on rebuilding
Answer: c) Irrevocably altered by the disaster
10.What is Ghosh's tone throughout the essay "Town by the Sea"?
a) Humorous
b) Reflective and somber
c) Critical and analytical
d) Optimistic and cheerful
Answer: b) Reflective and somber

Long Answers Questions:

1. Analyze how Amitav Ghosh portrays the impact of the 2004 Indian Ocean tsunami on the town of Galle in his essay "Town by the Sea."

In "Town by the Sea," Amitav Ghosh poignantly portrays the devastating impact of the 2004 Indian Ocean tsunami on the town of Galle, Sri Lanka. Ghosh's narrative captures both the physical and emotional aftermath of the disaster, painting a vivid picture of a town that was once serene and picturesque but is now marked by destruction and loss.

Ghosh begins by reminiscing about Galle before the tsunami, describing it as a peaceful coastal town with a rich cultural heritage and natural beauty. This serene image is shattered by the tsunami, which he describes as an "inconceivable disaster" that swept away lives, homes, and the very essence of the town. Ghosh uses detailed descriptions to convey the extent of the destruction, emphasizing how the landscape and the lives of the inhabitants were irrevocably changed.

The essay also delves into the emotional impact of the disaster on the survivors. Ghosh recounts the stories of those who lost their loved ones, their homes, and their sense of security in a matter of moments. He portrays the collective grief of the community, highlighting the deep sense of loss that permeates the town. Ghosh's reflections on the fragility of life and the vulnerability of coastal communities add a layer of depth to the essay, making it not just a recounting of a tragic event but a meditation on the human condition.

Furthermore, Ghosh explores the broader implications of the tsunami, touching on themes of environmental change and human resilience. He reflects on the unpredictability of such disasters and the challenges faced by those trying to rebuild their lives. The essay raises important questions about humanity's relationship with nature, particularly in the context of climate change and the increasing frequency of extreme weather events.

Ghosh's portrayal of the impact of the tsunami on Galle is both vivid and profound. Through his detailed descriptions and personal reflections, he captures the full scope of the disaster's effects, not just on the physical landscape but on the collective psyche of the town's inhabitants. "Town by the Sea" is a powerful reminder of the devastating consequences of natural disasters and the enduring human spirit in the face of overwhelming tragedy.

2. Discuss the themes of memory and loss in Amitav Ghosh's "Town by the Sea."

In "Town by the Sea," Amitav Ghosh intricately weaves the themes of memory and loss throughout his narrative, using them to explore the profound impact of the 2004 Indian Ocean tsunami on the town of Galle, Sri Lanka. These themes are central to Ghosh's reflections as he revisits a place he once knew well, only to find it transformed by disaster.

Memory plays a crucial role in Ghosh's essay, as he juxtaposes his recollections of Galle before the tsunami with the stark reality of the town in the aftermath of the disaster. He vividly recalls the town's beauty, its historic charm, and the warmth of its people. These memories serve as a poignant contrast to the devastation he witnesses upon his return. Ghosh's reflections on the past underscore the fragility of human experiences and how quickly they can be altered by unforeseen events.

The theme of loss is deeply intertwined with memory in Ghosh's essay. The tsunami's destruction is not just physical but also emotional, as it erases the familiar landmarks and routines that once defined the lives of Galle's inhabitants. Ghosh captures the profound sense of loss experienced by the survivors, who not only mourn the deaths of loved ones but also grieve the loss of their homes, their livelihoods, and their way of life. The essay portrays this loss as something that extends beyond the immediate aftermath, affecting the collective memory of the community and altering its identity.

Ghosh also reflects on the idea of collective memory and how the town's shared history has been reshaped by the disaster. The tsunami becomes a defining moment in the town's history, a marker that divides the past from the present. Ghosh suggests that the memories of the town before the tsunami are now tinged with sadness, as they are inextricably linked to the loss that followed. This blending of memory and loss highlights the complex emotions that arise in the wake of a tragedy, where the past is both cherished and mourned.

Moreover, Ghosh's exploration of memory and loss extends to the broader context of environmental change. He raises questions about the impermanence of human settlements and the vulnerability of coastal communities to natural disasters. The essay suggests that the memories of places like Galle are at risk of being lost as climate change leads to more frequent and severe environmental events.

"Town by the Sea" is a profound meditation on memory and loss, using the 2004 tsunami as a lens through which to explore these themes. Ghosh's reflections on the town of Galle, its people, and its history offer a poignant commentary on the human experience, highlighting the enduring impact of loss on individual and collective memory.

3. Examine the role of nature in Amitav Ghosh's essay "Town by the Sea" and its connection to the theme of human vulnerability.

In "Town by the Sea," Amitav Ghosh presents nature as both a source of beauty and a force of destruction, highlighting the complex relationship between humans and the natural world. This duality is central to the essay, as it underscores the theme of human vulnerability in the face of nature's unpredictable power.

Ghosh begins the essay by describing the natural beauty of Galle, a coastal town in Sri Lanka. The town's serene environment, with its scenic coastline and tranquil sea, is depicted as an integral part of its charm. This idyllic portrayal of nature serves as a backdrop to the lives of the town's inhabitants, who have built their homes and livelihoods in harmony with the surrounding environment.

However, this harmony is shattered by the 2004 Indian Ocean tsunami, a catastrophic natural event that transforms the peaceful sea into a deadly force. Ghosh's detailed account of the tsunami's impact on Galle vividly illustrates the destructive power of nature, which can upend lives and landscapes in an instant. The essay captures the sheer scale of the disaster, with nature's wrath leaving behind a trail of devastation that no human effort could have prevented or mitigated.

The role of nature in the essay is closely linked to the theme of human vulnerability. Ghosh reflects on how the tsunami exposed the fragility of human settlements, particularly those along coastlines that are susceptible to such natural disasters. The essay suggests that despite technological advancements and modern infrastructure, humans remain at the mercy of nature's unpredictable forces. This vulnerability is not only physical but also psychological, as the disaster leaves deep emotional scars on the survivors.

Ghosh also touches on the broader implications of environmental change, hinting at the increasing frequency and intensity of natural disasters due to climate change. This connection between nature and human vulnerability raises important questions about the sustainability of coastal communities and the need for greater awareness and preparedness in the face of environmental threats. Ghosh's reflections suggest that the relationship between humans and nature is one of delicate balance, where the natural world can be both nurturing and destructive.

Nature plays a central role in "Town by the Sea," serving as both a backdrop to human life and a powerful force that can disrupt it at any moment. Ghosh's essay explores the vulnerability of humans in the face of nature's unpredictability, offering a sobering reminder of the limitations of human control over the environment. Through his depiction of the tsunami's impact on Galle, Ghosh underscores the need for a deeper understanding of and respect for the natural world.

***

Unit 4
Language Component
Punctuation

Punctuation refers to the marks used in writing to separate sentences and clarify meaning. Correct punctuation is essential for clear communication.

1. Period (.)

- **Purpose:** Ends a declarative sentence or a statement.
- **Example:**
  - She went to the store.
  - The meeting starts at 10 a.m.

2. Comma (,)

- **Purpose:** Separates elements in a list, connects independent clauses with a conjunction, and sets off introductory elements, among other uses.
- **Examples:**
  - I bought apples, oranges, and bananas.
  - She was tired, so she went to bed early.
  - After the movie, we went for dinner.

3. Question Mark (?)

- **Purpose:** Ends a direct question.
- **Examples:**
  - What time is it?
  - Are you coming to the party?

4. Exclamation Mark (!)

- **Purpose:** Expresses strong emotion or emphasis.

- **Examples:**

  - Watch out!

  - That's amazing!

5. Semicolon (;)

- **Purpose:** Connects closely related independent clauses or separates items in a list when those items contain commas.

- **Examples:**

  - She loves to read; her favorite author is Jane Austen.

  - We visited Paris, France; Rome, Italy; and Berlin, Germany.

6. Colon (:)

- **Purpose:** Introduces a list, explanation, or quotation.

- **Examples:**

  - He had three choices: stay home, go to the party, or visit his grandparents.

  - She said it best: "Hard work pays off."

7. Quotation Marks (" ")

- **Purpose:** Encloses direct speech, quotations, or titles of short works like articles or poems.

- **Examples:**

  - She said, "I'll be there soon."

o   Have you read "The Road Not Taken" by Robert
       Frost?

8. Apostrophe (')

- **Purpose:** Shows possession or forms contractions.

- **Examples:**

     o   Sara's book is on the table. (Possession)

     o   It's a beautiful day. (Contraction of "It is")

     o   The teachers' lounge is upstairs. (Possession for
         plural noun)

9. Dash (—)

- **Purpose:** Indicates a break in thought or adds emphasis,
  often more dramatic than a comma.

- **Examples:**

     o   He was thinking about the game—then he heard the
         doorbell ring.

     o   The decision—though difficult—was the right one.

10. Hyphen (-)

- **Purpose:** Joins words in compound terms or splits a word
  at the end of a line.

- **Examples:**

     o   Well-known author

     o   Mother-in-law

     o   The quick-thinking doctor saved her life.

Exercise

Add the appropriate punctuation to the following sentences:

1. I cant believe its already December where did the year go

2. She bought a new dress shoes and a handbag for the party

3. My brother who lives in Chicago is visiting us next weekend

4. Did you know that the Earth revolves around the sun

5. After the long meeting we decided to go out for dinner

6. The teacher asked what is the capital of France

7. My favorite books include Pride and Prejudice 1984 and The Great Gatsby

8. Its important to be on time the meeting starts at 9 am

9. He shouted Watch out theres a car coming

10. We need the following items milk bread eggs and butter

11. The authors book which was published last year became a bestseller

12. She said Ill be there at 3 pm but she didnt arrive until 4

13. The conference was held in New York City on July 23 2023

14. The winners of the contest are Sarah James and Emily

15. The house on the corner the one with the red door is for sale

16. She was late however she still managed to catch the train

17. The quick brown fox jumps over the lazy dog

18. Youll need to bring a tent sleeping bag and a flashlight for
    the camping trip

19. The sign read No parking beyond this point

20. Its a well known fact that smoking is harmful to your health

Answer Key

1. I can't believe it's already December! Where did the year
    go?

2. She bought a new dress, shoes, and a handbag for the party.

3. My brother, who lives in Chicago, is visiting us next
    weekend.

4. Did you know that the Earth revolves around the sun?

5. After the long meeting, we decided to go out for dinner.

6. The teacher asked, "What is the capital of France?"

7. My favorite books include *Pride and Prejudice*, *1984*, and
    The Great Gatsby.

8. It's important to be on time; the meeting starts at 9 a.m.

9. He shouted, "Watch out! There's a car coming!"

10. We need the following items: milk, bread, eggs, and butter.

11. The author's book, which was published last year, became
    a bestseller.

12. She said, "I'll be there at 3 p.m.," but she didn't arrive until
    4.

13. The conference was held in New York City on July 23,
    2023.

14. The winners of the contest are Sarah, James, and Emily.

15. The house on the corner—the one with the red door—is for sale.

16. She was late; however, she still managed to catch the train.

17. The quick brown fox jumps over the lazy dog.

18. You'll need to bring a tent, sleeping bag, and a flashlight for the camping trip.

19. The sign read, "No parking beyond this point."

20. It's a well-known fact that smoking is harmful to your health.

***

Articles

Articles are words used before nouns to indicate whether the nouns are specific or general. In English, there are three articles: **"a,"** **"an,"** and **"the."**

1. Definite Article: "The"

- **Usage:** "The" is used when referring to a specific noun that is known to the reader or listener.

- **Examples:**

    o **The cat** that I saw yesterday is back in the garden.

    o **The book** on the table is mine.

    o **The sun** rises in the east.

Explanation:

- In the first sentence, "the cat" refers to a specific cat that both the speaker and the listener are aware of.

100

- In the second sentence, "the book" refers to a particular book that is already identified or known.

- In the third sentence, "the sun" refers to the one and only sun, making it specific.

2. Indefinite Articles: "A" and "An"

- **Usage:** "A" and "An" are used before singular, countable nouns when the noun is being mentioned for the first time or when it's not specifically known to the reader or listener.

- **"A"** is used before words that begin with a consonant sound.

- **"An"** is used before words that begin with a vowel sound (a, e, i, o, u).

- **Examples:**

  - She wants to buy **a car**. (Any car, not a specific one)

  - Can you bring **an umbrella**? (Any umbrella, not a specific one)

  - He is **a doctor**. (Refers to the profession, not a specific doctor)

  - She ate **an apple** for breakfast. (Any apple, not a specific one)

Explanation:

- In the first sentence, "a car" refers to any car, not a specific one.

- In the second sentence, "an umbrella" refers to any umbrella, not a specific one.

- In the third sentence, "a doctor" refers to his profession in general.

- In the fourth sentence, "an apple" refers to any apple, not a particular one.

3. Zero Article (No Article)

- **Usage:** Sometimes, no article is used before nouns, especially with plural and uncountable nouns when talking in a general sense.

- **Examples:**

  - **Water** is essential for life. (Uncountable noun, general statement)

  - **Cats** are great pets. (Plural noun, general statement)

  - **She likes to read** books. (Plural noun, general preference)

Explanation:

- In the first sentence, "water" is uncountable, and the sentence refers to water in general.

- In the second sentence, "cats" is a plural noun, referring to all cats in general.

- In the third sentence, "books" is a plural noun, indicating a general preference for reading.

Exercise

Fill in the blanks with articles:

1. I saw ____ dog in the park. ____ dog was chasing a ball.

2. She is ____ excellent teacher.

3. Can you hand me ____ book on the table?

4. We need to buy ____ new car.

5. He is eating ____ apple and drinking ____ glass of water.

6. ____ sun sets in the west.

7. My brother is ____ engineer.

8. Do you have ____ pencil I can borrow?

9. She wants to be ____ artist.

10. I met ____ old friend yesterday.

11. We visited ____ museum during our trip.

12. She loves to play ____ piano.

13. ____ earth orbits around ____ sun.

14. ____ books on the shelf are mine.

15. ____ elephant is ____ large animal.

16. She doesn't have ____ job right now.

17. I want to become ____ doctor in the future.

18. ____ water in this bottle is cold.

19. They live in ____ big house near ____ river.

20. Can you name ____ highest mountain in the world?

Answer Key

1. I saw a dog in the park. The dog was chasing a ball.

2. She is an excellent teacher.

3. Can you hand me the book on the table?

4. We need to buy a new car.

5. He is eating an apple and drinking a glass of water.

6. The sun sets in the west.

7. My brother is an engineer.

8. Do you have a pencil I can borrow?

9. She wants to be an artist.

10. I met an old friend yesterday.

11. We visited a museum during our trip.

12. She loves to play the piano.

13. The earth orbits around the sun.

14. The books on the shelf are mine.

15. An elephant is a large animal.

16. She doesn't have a job right now.

17. I want to become a doctor in the future.

18. The water in this bottle is cold.

19. They live in a big house near the river.

20. Can you name the highest mountain in the world?

Subject- Verb Agreement

Subject-Verb Agreement is a fundamental rule in English grammar that requires the verb to match the subject in number (singular or plural) and person (first, second, or third).

Basic Rules of Subject-Verb Agreement:

1. **Singular subjects take singular verbs.**

    o Example: **She runs** every morning.

       ▪ *Explanation:* "She" is a singular subject, so the verb "runs" is also singular.

2. **Plural subjects take plural verbs.**

    o Example: **They run** every morning.

       ▪ *Explanation:* "They" is a plural subject, so the verb "run" is also plural.

3. **Subjects joined by "and" take a plural verb.**

    o Example: **Tom and Jerry are** best friends.

       ▪ *Explanation:* "Tom" and "Jerry" together form a plural subject, so the verb "are" is plural.

4. **When two subjects are joined by "or" or "nor," the verb agrees with the subject closest to it.**

    o Example: Either the teacher or the students **are** responsible.

    o Example: Neither the students nor the teacher **is** available.

       ▪ *Explanation:* In the first example, "students" is closest to the verb, so the verb is plural. In the second example, "teacher" is closest to the verb, so the verb is singular.

5. **When the subject is a collective noun, it can take either a singular or plural verb, depending on whether the group is acting as one unit or as individuals.**

   - Example: **The team is** winning. (acting as a single unit)

   - Example: **The team are** arguing among themselves. (acting as individuals)

     - *Explanation:* In the first sentence, "team" is seen as a single entity, so the verb is singular. In the second sentence, "team" members are acting individually, so the verb is plural.

6. **"There" and "Here" are not subjects. The subject follows the verb, and the verb agrees with the subject.**

   - Example: **There is** a book on the table.

   - Example: **There are** many books on the table.

     - *Explanation:* In the first sentence, the subject "book" is singular, so the verb "is" is singular. In the second sentence, the subject "books" is plural, so the verb "are" is plural.

7. **Indefinite pronouns like "everyone," "each," "either," "neither," "nobody," etc., take singular verbs.**

   - Example: **Everyone is** invited to the party.

   - Example: **Neither** of the options **is** suitable.

- - *Explanation:* "Everyone" and "neither" are treated as singular, so the verbs "is" in both sentences are singular.

8. **Subjects that express an amount, such as "one-third of," "a lot of," "some of," etc., can be singular or plural depending on what they are referring to.**

   - Example: **A lot of** the cake **is** gone. (refers to a singular noun "cake")

   - Example: **A lot of** the students **are** absent. (refers to a plural noun "students")

     - *Explanation:* The verb agrees with the noun that follows the phrase.

9. **Titles of books, movies, and other works are singular, even if they are plural in form.**

   - Example: **"The Chronicles of Narnia"** **is** a popular series.

     - *Explanation:* Although "Chronicles" is plural, the title as a whole is treated as a singular entity, so the verb "is" is singular.

10. **Some nouns, although plural in form, are treated as singular.**

    - Example: **Mathematics is** a difficult subject.

    - Example: **The news was** shocking.

      - *Explanation:* "Mathematics" and "news" look plural but are treated as singular, so they take singular verbs.

Common Mistakes and How to Avoid Them:

- **Mistake:** The list of items **are** on the table.

    o **Correction:** The list of items **is** on the table.

        ▪ *Explanation:* The subject is "list," which is singular, not "items," so the verb should be "is."

- **Mistake:** Each of the students **have** a book.

    o **Correction:** Each of the students **has** a book.

        ▪ *Explanation:* "Each" is singular, so the verb should be "has."

- **Mistake:** The data **was** analyzed.

    o **Correction:** The data **were** analyzed.

        ▪ *Explanation:* "Data" is plural, so the verb should be "were." (Note: In formal contexts, "data" is often treated as plural, though in everyday usage, it can be singular.)

Exercise

Exercise: Choose the correct verb form that agrees with the subject in each sentence.

1. The dog ____________ (bark) loudly every night.

2. Sarah, along with her friends, ____________ (go) to the concert last weekend.

3. Neither of the boys ____________ (like) spicy food.

4. Each of the books ____________ (have) a different cover design.

5. The committee members ____________ (disagree) on the budget proposal.

Answer Key:

1. barks

2. went

3. likes

4. has

5. disagree

Prepositions

A preposition is a word that shows the relationship between a noun (or pronoun) and other words in a sentence. It typically indicates direction, place, time, or introduces an object.

Common Types of Prepositions:

- **Prepositions of Place:** Indicate location.

    o   Examples: in, on, at, under, over, between

    o   Example Sentences:

        ▪   The book is **on** the table.

        ▪   She sat **between** her friends.

- **Prepositions of Time:** Indicate when something happens.

    o   Examples: at, on, in, before, after, during

    o   Example Sentences:

        ▪   The meeting is **at** 10 a.m.

- We will visit them **in** December.

- **Prepositions of Direction:** Indicate movement towards something.

    o Examples: to, into, onto, through, towards

    o Example Sentences:

        - She walked **to** the store.

        - He jumped **into** the pool.

- **Prepositions of Manner:** Indicate how something is done.

    o Examples: by, with, without, like

    o Example Sentences:

        - She solved the problem **with** ease.

        - He traveled **by** train.

Preposition + Noun (or Pronoun): Prepositions are usually followed by a noun or pronoun, which is called the object of the preposition.

- Example: The cat is **under the table**. (Here, "under" is the preposition, and "the table" is the object.)

Prepositional Phrases: A prepositional phrase starts with a preposition and ends with the object of the preposition.

- Example: The keys are **on the kitchen counter**.

- Function: Prepositional phrases can function as adjectives or adverbs.

    o Adjective: The man **with the red hat** is my uncle. (Describes "man")

- o   Adverb: She ran **through the park**. (Describes "ran")

Exercise

A. Fill in the blanks with the correct prepositions:

1. The cat is hiding __________ the couch. (under, in, on)

2. We will meet __________ Friday. (in, at, on)

3. The plane flew __________ the clouds. (over, under, between)

4. He has been living here __________ five years. (since, for, during)

5. The kids are playing __________ the garden. (at, on, in)

B. Identify the prepositional phrases in the following sentences:

1. She arrived at the station on time.

2. The book on the shelf is mine.

3. They traveled by car to the countryside.

4. The meeting was held in the conference room.

5. He walked through the park in the evening.

Answer Key:

A. Fill in the blanks:

1. under

2. on

3. over

4. for

5. in

B. Identify the prepositional phrases:

1. at the station, on time

2. on the shelf

3. by car, to the countryside

4. in the conference room

5. through the park, in the evening

***

www.ingramcontent.com/pod-product-compliance
Lightning Source LLC
LaVergne TN
LVHW051446170726
843492LV00002B/579